Thatastu

Kalyanam

by

Savitri Namana

Cover illustration by Niloufer Wadia

DEDICATION

This book is dedicated to Akka and Divya, whose sense of sisterhood is so strong that not only do I take complete advantage of their patience in listening to my stories, but also find inspiration in their enthusiasm and willingness to hear more.

It is nectar to a storyteller's soul.

The gently shut silver eye glistened with the last stroke of the brush. Stanley ducked his head under the hood of the seven-headed stone snake and leaned over to brush the back of the 7-foot tall *lingam*. He leaned precariously over the artifact to maintain his balance while standing on the small and narrow wooden bench, making sure he did not place his feet on the scared, or rather divine, object. His Indian associate and chief translator, Nagabushnam, had warned that even the thought of stepping on the *lingam* would get him in trouble with people and god! The short, *panchi-clad* man stood beside him with hands clasped, eyes shut, and reciting prayers.

Only last week, he and Nagabhushanam made this amazing, rather unexpected discovery during their excavation. Originally commissioned to dig up buried and forgotten treasures, Stanley had no hope of ever finding anything till the day he heard the loud clang of metal striking metal.

What they had initially considered a sole-standing artifact turned out to be a whole temple complex. For an archaeologist, that was equivalent to an amassed wealth. Money was not an issue for Stanley, though. He was loaded with it. As the older son of the late Earl of Whittamore, Stanley had inherited the fortune and the title. But, his interest never lay in the estate. Successful as he was at running it, Stanley found his calling with the buried pasts and less explored parts of the world.

He had approached the Society of Antiquaries of London to pursue his interest and could have easily bought a berth, but that was not how he wanted it. He soon discovered that the society's political environment and geographical limitations were not to his taste. So he decided to become a worthy explorer on his professor's advice before settling for a place in the societies.

His quest to prove himself and a thirst for the long forgotten had him board the ship of the East India Company and travel the breath of a nation that had him fascinated enough to set up a house in the country. India amazed Stanley. He had heard stories about this wealthy nation of the Rajas and Mughals but what he heard was not even close to what he saw. It was a different world in itself. He had traveled with the Archeological survey for the first three years in this country before he branched out by himself. Little did he know that he would be called a treasure finder rather than an archeologist. Interestingly, the Indians were as fascinated with a white man seeking opportunities as he was with the culture and landscape of this country. People either obliged him with the kind of work he sought or pointed him in the direction of a possibility. While working on an attempt to restore a long-neglected estate, Stanley stumbled upon a room full of treasures. And that is how his name had traveled, as the *Sahib* with a golden hand. Although he made little of his newfound fame, he would not let go of the opportunities it provided. Like Nagabushanam had once said, "First time you can say coincidence. A second time? Lucky maybe. But if it happened a third time, my fair friend, it is a divine intervention!"

Stanley had laughed at the time. But after this find, he was compelled to believe his Indian friend.

The roar of the thunder vibrated in the small enclosure, and the lightning that lit the sky reflected in the silver eye. Stanley stepped off the stool and dusted his hands. "Right!" He heaved, "Some water and it will shine as new"

Nagabushanam cringed, "Not IT! He. He will shine" He frowned at the ignorant white man.

"Sorry," Stanley folded his hands the Indian way.

"He. Shiva, right?"

"Yes"

"Ok. Shall we start?"

"No," A tall man spoke, gentle and firm, from the small entryway. Although dressed in the same manner as Nagabhushanam, the older gentleman's clothes were of a finer make than the young man's. Neela Nandana Seshadri Swamy, the village headman and lord of the very land that Stanley excavated, carried his tall frame with an attitude befitting a royal. Yet, his eyes were filled with awe as he laid eyes on the Shiva *lingam*. He held his hands in a *namaskaram* and bowed his head in reverence. He muttered a prayer under his breath and then raised his head "I am blessed.." he said, turning to Stanley, "that the lord found my land befitting for his stay." He gently clapped his nephew, Nagabhushanam, on his shoulders and then shook Stanley's hand. "You do have golden hands, Stanley *garu*!" he addressed Stanley with respect. Seshadri Swamy was a man fascinated with words. Written and spoken. So when this young man approached him with interest in the excavation, Swamy obliged. It was an opportunity for both of them to indulge in what they loved. For As a young man, he traveled across Bharat learning languages.

"Well, it was Na-bush-nam who told us where to dig. It is him you have to thank first." Stanley said.

"Of course! Of course!" Seshadri Swamy turned to his nephew and congratulated the young man in their native language, Telugu. He invited the two young men for dinner that night, but Stanley politely refused. After the intense, spicy experience the last time he accepted a dinner invitation, Stanley had no intention of answering nature's bottom-burning calls for the next few days.

Streaks of lightning illuminated the sky, revealing the dark, heavy clouds. Stanley raised his voice high enough to be heard over the rumbling thunder. "We have to clear up the area!! The rocks have to be stacked!! The soil is still loose and will flood if it rains!!"

"Yes.Yes.I will send my men to do it!" The older man raised his voice too. "The village priest will tell us what to do!"

"The priest?!" Stanley looked at the ruins, confused. "The priest digs?"

Sheshadri Swamy laughed. "No. No. He will..he will.." He racked his limited knowledge of English for an appropriate word, "clean the lord and see to the worship." Noting Stanley's blank look, he continued, "That is not just stone Stanley *garu*. He is our god. He needs to be cleaned and..and brought to life. And we have to do it the right way. The priest will tell us how and when to do it."

Stanley did not understand how that would work. He did not like the idea of the area being trampled upon before recordings were made. But he also knew not to interfere with divinity. "Do you happen to have any old records of your family's lands and estates other than the paper that you gave us?" He asked the older man. "It would be good to create a record on how and when this temple was constructed."

Seshadri Swamy walked up to one of the four pillars closest to him and ran his hand over the carvings. Nagabushanam walked over with an oil lamp and held it closer to the pillar. The two murmured something in Telugu and then turned to Stanley.

"I have not seen these carvings in our village, but it looks familiar. I cannot remember where I saw them." Seshadri Swamy put a finger to his forehead. A few seconds later, he signaled Nagabhushanam, "Speak to Mallayya. His family has been making statues for temples. His grandfather might recognize the carvings" He turned around to Stanley, "I will see what papers I have about the temple. My uncle will also know."

Stanley shrugged his shoulders and questioned the smiling man, "Are you not disappointed that we did not find any treasures?"

Seshadri Swamy shook his head. "No. A treasure would have added to what I have, Stanley *garu*. I have enough. But his.." he said, looking at the *lingam,* "blessings I needed. He has blessed me now!" misty-eyed, he bowed down to the lord.

Stanley glanced at Nagabhushanam, who signaled back with a simple nod.

The three men discussed the arrangements for the next day and left for home. On the way back, Nagabhushanam explained his uncle's words to Stanley. "He is a very good man. Very good to all the people also. He gives money to people when they need it and does not even charge interest. Not like the other money lenders. But god did not bless him properly!" He nodded sympathetically.

"What do you mean?" Stanley asked.

"You see, uncle is very rich. But nobody will marry his girls."

"Why?"

"Because Prabhavathi has *Kuja Dosham*, and Tharani can't marry before her *Akka*."

"Khoja what?!" a puzzled Stanley asked, unable to even pronounce the word. Not surprisingly, all the Indian languages he encountered felt more like tongue twisters than actual communicative words.

"Not *Khoja! Kuja. Kuja Dosham.*" Nagabhushanam stressed with a hand gesture. Noting Stanley's blank expression, he explained, "Prabhavathi has a strong influence of a planet on her birth star. That is not good for her husband. He can even die after marrying her. That is why nobody wants to marry her even though she is very beautiful. Nobody wants to die!"

"So she is never going to marry?"

"No. No. She can marry. But only to a man who also has *Kuja Dosham*."

Stanley raised his brows. "That way, they both die?"

Nagabhushanam laughed. "No. No. It will be good for both of them."

"Hmm." Stanley nodded his head in a contemplative manner. Weird are ways of the world. "Why can't the other daughter marry? What problem does she have?"

"Tharani? She does not have any problem. Good girl she is. Bad luck that she is younger to Prabhavathi. The family priest predicted that if the younger girl was married before, the older, it will bring bad luck to the whole family!"

"And you believed him?"

"Of course!" Nagabhushanam nodded vigorously.
"Everything he said till now has come true."
Stanley smirked. "Poor girl! It is a pity that she has to suffer."
"Ooh, don't pity her," Nagabhushanam gently warned Stanley. "Now that god is with my uncle, everything will be fine."
"Are you sure?"
The thunder rumbled in the sky again. "Of course!"
The young man differed, "Just you see how things will turn out."

2

"I knew it! The moment I saw him, I knew that our troubles are now gone," Sheshadri Swamy beamed at his wife, who was shedding tears of happiness. He held his hands in a Namaste and looked up at the bright sky through the wide opening in his courtyard. *"He has blessed us, Gowri. He has finally heard our prayers."* He said, *"What can I do to show my gratitude, my Lord?!"* He asked. A tear rolled down his cheek. Not one to display his emotions, today Swamy did not want to contain them. What a lovely day it had been!

The signs were there right from when he, and his wife, Gowri Devi, visited the temple site first thing in the morning. A calming fragrance and amber light had emanated from the small enclosure. Not only had the priest cleaned the idol and *garba gudi,* but he had also decorated the entire area with flowers. How divine it had looked! The rubble and boulders were shoved aside and stacked enough to create a small walkway down the steep slope. With villagers being busy with crop harvesting Seshadri Swamy could not get enough men to clear the area as Stanley had requested. Last heard, Stanley and Nagabhushanam had done most of the removing themselves, fearing that all the footfall would loosen the ground around the excavation.

Nagabhushanam was even present inside the *Garba gudi* when the older couple arrived. As soon as Shesadiri Swamy walked in, a beaming Nagabhushanam came up to him, *"I have some really good news for you, uncle!!"* He said.

Shesadiri Swamy smiled at his nephew. *"Shall we do the pooja first? Then you can tell me what is making you so happy"* he patted the young man on his shoulder.

Unable to hold his excitement Nagabhushanam went around to his aunt and whispered into her ear. Within seconds the frown on Gowri Devi's face changed to a wide smile. She began to bubble with as much emotion as her nephew-by-marriage. The feelings were contagious, and it was, initially, an effort for Sehsadiri Swamy to concentrate on the prayers that were to instill life into the lingam.

Nagabhushanam hovered around like a bee. He fetched this, corrected that, and dusted his dhoti. It was not until his father and Stanley walked in that Nagabhushanam quietened down following a stern look from his father.

"Your son is jumping around as if his bum is on fire," Shesadiri Swamy greeted his brother-in-law

after the pooja was done. *"What happened to him? Is he getting married?"*

Venkatesh, who looked like a much older version of his son, grasped Sheshadiri Swamy's arms and smiled heartily. *"With god's blessings, it will be your daughters who will be getting married, Swamy!"* He said.

"What do you mean?" Shesadiri frowned.

"I *was at Thirupathi Rao's house yesterday. His brother-in-law was visiting him, and so was his son. We talked about this and that, and then he told me his son has kujadosham too."*

Swamy frowned. Not wanting to voice his suspicion, he waited for Venkataiah to complete.

Venkataiah did. *"I mentioned Prabhavathi, and they want to meet you, Swamy."* He beamed. *"Thirupathi Rao and his wife spoke so highly of you and your girls that this match is all set. The meeting is just a formality."*

"But the boy..." Swamy began to question.

"You think I would get my niece an alliance that is not worthy of your stature. The boy is a good man. The family has a good name and are the Zamindars of the village. Coconut farms, Mango groves, rice fields, and cotton farms. You name it, and they have it. Janardhan is their oldest son and is a just man. He reminded me of you when you were younger, Swamy. Talk to them, and you will know."

Seshadri Swamy was speechless for a moment. Having stepped out of the *Garbha Gudi*, Swamy turned around and bowed to the deity in reverence. *"Swamy.."* Venkataiah spoke again, *"If all goes well..."* He hesitated a little *"I might sound a little selfish, but.."*

"But?" Swamy smiled at his brother-in-law *"Bawa.."* he addressed him traditionally, *"why the hesitation between us?"*

Venkataiah shook his head *"No.No. Now is not the time. We have a lot of things to prepare for. They will be coming in the afternoon. Shall we go?"*

"Yes. Yes." Swamy said, heading up the steep slope on which stones were arranged to create somewhat rocky and unsteady steps.

"Careful," Stanley called out when Swamy's foot slipped on a stone. He had been watching everything from a distance. With all the people talking in Telugu, Stanley was not privy to all the fuss. Still, looking at their manners and happy faces, he understood Swamy's sentiments.

Swamy steadied himself. "I am fine. I am fine." He smiled a little sheepishly. "I should not be hurrying."

"Yes. You should not be." Stanley helped Nagabhushanam push some small rocks out of the way. "The soil is still loose. We tried to beat it down, but with all the people constantly walking up and down, it is coming apart," he complained. "Is there really no way we can stop the people from coming."

"I am sorry, Stanley garu. All the men are busy with harvesting. I will try to send some men."

"What about the people coming to see the Lingam?" Stanley persisted.

Swamy patted Stanley's shoulder. "Everybody wants to see the lord Stanley garu.."

"But.."

Swamy gently raised his hand. "I will tell people to wait, but I cannot stop a whole village from wanting to pray their respects, Stanley garu. He belongs to everybody. We can again start work once the people stop coming. I will pay you for the extra days, Stanley garu."

Dark clouds rolled over them and blocked out the sun, giving the morning a grey hue. Stanley sighed. "As long as your lord does not pour down the sky on us." Swamy smiled as usual and left for his house.

Once Swamy and Gowri returned home, the whole house burst into a bustle. The house was dusted, the silver taken out, the cows milked, swèets made, and the girls dressed in silk.

"What do you mean I have to stay in the kitchen?" Tharani had questioned her mother.

"It means you have to stay in the kitchen till everybody leaves," Gowri Devi chided her younger daughter while pulling out a Saree from the metal storage box under the bed.

"Amma!!" Tharani huffed, sat on the high wooden bed, and pouted like a miffed child.

"Speak softly!" Gowri frowned. *"God is finally looking down kindly at us. I will not have you destroy*

*that with your silliness. No. Now be quiet. I have to
get your sister ready."*
Seshadri Swamy walked in at the exact moment to
find his youngest daughter sitting miffed. He walked
up to her, smiled, and held her chin tenderly.
*"You are my good girl, right? Listen to your Amma
once, and I will get those anklets made for you."*
The 18-year-old's face broke into a smile, and her doe
eyes sparkled. *"Just like the ones I showed you in the
temple?!"*
"Exactly like those ones."
"And a new nose ring?!"
"And a new nose ring!" Seshadri laughed at his
daughter's eagerness
"And..."
*"And new bangles and necklace and armlets and
everything!"* He said, *"Now go and get me some fruits
to eat. Naana is very hungry."*
Tharani clapped her hands and jumped off the bed. *"I
will go and come like lightning!!"* She sprinted out of
the room!
*"You should not indulge her so much. What is the
need to buy more gold now? I got everything made
for both girls just two years ago."*
Seshadri Swamy sat on the bed and pulled his wife
closer. *"If I don't indulge my daughters, who should I
spoil? Your father's daughter?"* He teased his wife.
Gowri Devi slapped her husband's hand away and sat
down beside him, holding a red silk saree. She ran her
hand gently over it. Tears filled her eyes. *"I just pray*

to the lord that everything goes well. God only knows how earnestly I have prayed for this. Our girls deserve better. Tharani is very carefree and does not take things to her heart. But Prabhavathi. She is very sensitive. She has endured a lot. I know how she feels when her friends meet and talk about their husbands and children. My heart breaks every time people say such things about our girls." She sniffed. *"That girl? That Parmeshwari's girl? She cannot cook to save her own life. And. And that Annapoorna's girl is cock eyed. Prasanna's daughter has a lisp. Chandrika's daughter can't walk straight. Yet, all of them got married. And my girls? My lovely girls. They can cook for 50 people. They know how to keep the house clean. They can run the house very efficiently. They sing so beautifully. Yes, Tharani is a little darker, but I have not seen another child with such lovely eyes."* Gowri Devi gently cracked her knuckles along the sides of her forehead, a traditional way of breaking a jinx on somebody.

Swamy patted his wife's hand. *"I have a good feeling about it, Gowri. It was only a matter of time. That is all. I know how it has been for us. Having two unmarried young girls. Now, with god's grace, everything will be good."*

And it was. Seshadri Swamy's sister and brother-in-law, Venkataiah, had come to help with the preparations and be part of the formal meeting for the alliance. Venkataiah did most of the talking on behalf of Swamy, and like he had informed, it was a mere formality. One look at Prabhavathi and the matter was sealed for the groom's party. The family astrologer priest was called in to appoint a date for the marriage. It was then that Venkataiah interrupted and asked Swamy for Tharani's hand in marriage for his son, Nagabhushanam.

Surprised as he was, an elated Swamy hugged his brother-in-law. *"This must be the happiest day of my life!"* he declared. And that was that. A month from now, both his daughters were to get married on the same day, at the same time.

3

"Are you not the sweetest bawa of all? Can you not take us there." Prabhavathi pleaded with her cousin, *"Everybody in the village has seen him except us. Please, bawa!"*

"I am the only bawa you have," Nagabhushanam said, looking away from Prabhavathi. It was difficult for him to say no to the girls. Being the oldest of the three, he was always the commander in chief for all their childhood games. What he spoke was the rule to be followed. Prabhavathi was obedient and followed what he said, but Tharani always did what she wanted. They had often quarreled on who was better, and Nagabhushanam always gave in to his little cousin. Today he saw a different Tharani. Peeping over her older sister's shoulder was a young, shy girl who seemed to blush at seeing him. Despite the shy smile, her doe-like eyes twinkled. The announcement of their wedding and the acceptance that they were to be husband and wife suddenly changed the way they behaved with each other. Nagabhushanam cleared his throat and focused on the flower in Tharani's

hair. *"Yesterday's rain collapsed the way we paved down to the temple. The mud is very slippery."* He looked up at the sky. The dark clouds, unnatural for the time of the year, loomed over the village. The air was humid, and rain was imminent. *"It is too dangerous for us to go now."*

"Oh, don't say that!" Prabhavathi folded her hands and pleaded, *"In two weeks, I will go away to my in-laws' place. After tomorrow I won't be allowed out of the house. Please bawa. Please take us there. Just one minute. I need to thank the lord. That is all. Please!"* Nagabhushanam contemplated. Prabhavathi was right. God knows when she will be able to come home again. But. He looked up at the sky again. *"Just two minutes, bawa,"* Tharani spoke shyly. *"Can we not thank him for the good fortune he has bestowed upon us?"* She smiled.

A wavering Nagabhushanam melted completely at that dainty smile. *"Ok. But we have to come back fast. We should reach home before the evening lamps are lit. Ok?"*

"Just give us five minutes. We will go and come in a flash." an excited Tharani pulled her older sister and ran through the back door into the house.

Fifteen minutes later, Nagabhushanam was still waiting at the end of the mud path leading to the back of his uncle's house. *"I should not have listened to these girls,"* he muttered. It had just begun to drizzle, and he began to doubt the rightness of what he was doing. He saw the two girls running, towards him, with trays of fruits and flowers in their hands. Thinking it would be a waste of time to even try and scold them, he rushed them into the hooded bullock cart and jumped onto the front. The girls had an earful of disciplinary words on the way to the temple. Although, that did not stop them from stepping into the pouring rain and running down the path to the temple, much against their cousin's warning and wishes.

"I am not going to turn away from his door," Tharani insisted when her to-be-husband noted that the path down was slippery with small waterways being formed. Prabhavathi was torn between her sister, tugging on her hand, and her cousin's glaring looks. *"We will leave right now, Tharani!"* his loud voice conveyed his displeasure. *"It is not safe. Come?"* He held out his hand. *"I promise I will bring you, girls, back here as soon as the rain stops,"* He tried to reason.

Tharani was not to be reasoned with, *"Tomorrow morning, we are being made the brides. We cannot come out of the house after that."* So saying, she pulled hard at Prabhavathi and went down the muddy path. A reluctant Nagabhushanam followed, mentally ascertaining his ability to control Tharani once they were married. Streaks of lightning lit up the dark sky as the rain poured down relentlessly. The *Garba gudi* was dark and cool. The sisters walked over slowly to the Lingam and lit oil lamps on either side of the tall structure. They placed the flowers and proceeded to pray. Nagabhushanam grew restless. He looked over his shoulder at the small entryway and saw mud sliding down towards the enclosure.

"Hurry up! We must..." A loud thud along the side of the entrance startled the three of them.

Nagabhushanam ran out to see what had caused the sound. As he had feared..a giant boulder sitting at the edge of the dugout had rolled down with the mudslide. That was it. He ran into the enclosure and, grabbing the hands of both the girls, dragged them out into the rain. *"We are leaving now!"* he screamed against the rumbling sky.

"What the hell are you doing down there?!" Stanley shouted out to the Nagabhushanam from atop the dugout. He slid down the path and confronted the young man. "Why did you bring them here?!! Hurry up. The boulders are rolling down!"

Unable to see and hear clearly in the heavy downpour Nagabhushanam just nodded and pulled the girls along. He led while Stanley followed at the back of the group. Nagabhushanam tried pushing the girls ahead, but Prabhavathi could not hold onto anything and kept losing her footing. Nagabhushanam climbed on and pulled Prabhavathi along. Tharani held onto her sister's hand but lost her foot, and the three slid down again.

"Two at a time," Stanley said. "You pull her up," He instructed Nagabhushanam. "I will bring her along" he pointed at Tharani and extended his hand towards her. Tharani hesitated for a split second before placing her hand in his. They tried climbing up in different directions, and Nagabhushanam finally managed to pull Prabhavathi up. Looking down, the area was filling up with mud and water. "Come from the back of the temple!" Nagabhushanam screamed out to Stanley, who could still not pull himself up. Stanley pulled Tharani in that direction and almost reached the area when Nagabhushanam screamed out Tharani's name. Tharani turned around to see a huge boulder rolling down their way and screamed. Stanley pulled her quickly into the only way out of its path. The enclosure of the *Garba gudi*. So narrow was the escape before the vast boulder shut out the entrance that Tharani's free end of the saree *pallu* got trapped between the boulder and stone entryway. Tharani panicked and began to pull hard at her *pallu.*

"Stop! Stop!" Stanley spoke in a loud whisper. Looking at Tharani's half scared and half frowning face, he put up his hand, signaling her to stop the struggle. He pulled out a pocket knife and slit through the far end of the *pallu* trapped in the rock. Tharani held her shortened *pallu* in wide-eyed shock. Stanley shrugged his shoulders. "What? What should I do?" Though he understood what her surprise was about, he did not know how to convey that; that was the only thing he could think of. He turned around and looked at the place. Little light was glowing from the lamps the sisters had lit a while ago. He turned to the rock again. He ran his hand across the edge of the entryway. Not a wisp of air. The entrance was sealed rock solid. Tharani tapped her hand on the rock beside his and raised her brows at him. Stanley sighed. "I am sorry," he said and shook his head. Tharani shook her head sideways, not wanting to accept what Stanley conveyed, *"God! God!"* She held her head and looked around frantically. She ran to the back of the Lingam and knocked on the stonewall. Hearing only a solid thud, she came around and, pointing at the rear wall, looked questioningly at Stanley.

Stanley shook his head. The Garbha gudi was a stone enclosure with the entrance the only way in and out. The chamber offered little light, primarily from the small openings on the sides of the high and triangle-shaped ceiling.

Tears welled up in Tharani's eyes. She moved slowly towards the entrance and began pushing the rock. She was very focused and determined at the task. Stanley started to help, knowing all well the futility of the job. He did not want to discourage the girl. If she was determined, then he shall help her. God knows. A miracle might happen. He took a deep breath and pushed till the veins in his arms began to pop out. A good five minutes later, he heard Tharani sobbing.

 She stopped pushing and, leaning her head against the rock, began to hit it hard! The bangles on her hand broke and spluttered around.

'Stop! Stop it!" Stanley grabbed her hands when she did not listen to him.

"I deserve this! This has to happen to me! I should have listened to Bawa. But no. Why will I listen? Stubborn idiot I am!" Tharani looked at Stanley with red, tear laden eyes.

Girls, let alone crying girls, were not Stanley's comfort zone. Looking down at those tear-filled doe eyes made Stanley very uncomfortable in his own skin. He did not understand Tharani's words, but he understood the emotion. "Don"t..don't cry, please." he looked away. God! If only he could find a way out! "I...I will try. Though I am not sure how. But I am sure it will get better. It is not like we are going to die out of starvation here" He smiled gingerly at her. "We will most likely die of a cold," He said, looking down at their soaked clothes. It was then that they realized that he was still holding her hands.

Stanley let go and cleared his throat. "Sorry. I....I...did not..." He looked around and noticed the oil lamps still glowing at the Lingam walked over. He grabbed the cloth draped around the Lingam, poured a little oil over it, and lit it. He looked around for more fuel for the fire. Understanding the requirement, Tharani picked up the coconuts offered to God and began husking them to add to the fire. They finally sat down on either side of the cozy fire they had built.

After an awkward silence, Stanley cleared his throat and pointed at himself. "Stanley Patrick Whittamore," he introduced himself. He did not know Telugu, and it was pretty clear that she did not speak or even understand English. They were communicating merely by gestures and heightened emotions. Tharani's blank expression did not help improve their situation's awkwardness, which Stanley was finding difficult to ignore and accept.

A moment later, Tharani spoke gently, *"Tharani Sree."*

Stanley smiled " Well...I guess...we...just have to..wait and see..what will happen to us."

4

I am very sorry, uncle! Please, please forgive me!" Nagabhushanam cried. His tears had dried up, but the anguish he felt weighed heavy on his heart and his face. The past two days had been a living hell for him, and he suspected that was how he would feel for the rest of his life. Every time he closed his eyes, he could only see the image of the huge boulder rolling towards Tharani and crushing her to death. He fell at his uncle's feet. *"Please, uncle! Please! Beat me, uncle! Beat me! Kill me with your hands. At least that way, I can go to hell with peace. I deserve to die for my mistake. Please unc..."*

"Nagabhushanam," Swamy spoke in a steady voice. He swallowed hard before he continued, *"Crying like this won't get the work done. I.."* He stopped before choking on his words, *"I just want to see her"* Without looking back at his nephew Swamy began digging the last layer of mud surrounding the rock. How had this happened? Why did this happen? How could god have given him the greatest of joys and then taken it away, in a flash, even before the

happiness could sink in? Why did god do this to him? To his family? What had he ever done to deserve this kind of fate?

Swamy cleared his misty eyes. They had to keep going. It had rained the whole night on that fateful day. Much as Swamy and Nagabhushanam had tried to gather people and start digging immediately, the pouring rain made it difficult for people to even find their footing. Swamy had refused to leave his daughter in a muddy grave. He dug the same area repeatedly until Venkataiah pulled him away and restrained him. Swamy declined to return home and sat in the village temple praying all night. Gowri Devi had fainted at the news of her younger daughter's fate, and distressed as she was, Prabhavathi remained by her mother's side.

As soon as the rain stopped in the early hours of the following day, all the men in the village joined hands to dig out the temple complex. They were relentless at it. The temple elephants were brought in to pull out the huge boulders.

The whole village worked in batches until the wee hours of the second day, and it was now that they reached the boulder blocking the entrance to the *Garba gudi*. Gowri Devi, who rushed to the spot as soon as she could get her senses back, screamed at the sight of it. At the same time, Swamy noticed the free end of a muddy and battered sari *pallu* trapped between the boulder and the entrance. His face drained of blood. Swamy felt a lump forming in his throat. Nagabhushanam collapsed to his knees and began to sob loudly. The working men calmed into a mournful silence. It was some time before Swamy could hear the soft thumping. The village man close by leaned his head against the wall and listened, *"Somebody is in there!"* He said in a relieved voice.

Swamy dropped his tool and hurried to the wall. With a quiver in his voice, he spoke as loudly as possible: *"Tharani!..Ranamma!"*

"Naa..na," a faint voice replied.

The sound of his daughter's voice brought tears to Swamy's eyes. With a heavy sigh of relief, he sputtered, *"Ranamma! We are coming! A little patience, my child! Just a little while! We are here! Almost ...Ranamma?! We are coming! Are...are you alright?! Ranamma?!...Tharani?!"* Unable to hear his daughter's voice, Swamy began to panic and slammed the wall. He heard a muffled voice but could not make out what it was. He signaled Nagabhushanam to listen to what Stanley was saying. Nagabhushanam leaned against the stone wall.

"Wa...wall?...bre..break.. wall? Break wall?"

Swamy looked at the blouder. The temple wall is thinner than the boulder. He yelled to his men, *"Here*!" he pointed at the wall beside the blocked entrance. *"Strike here. Come! Fast!"* Swamy turned toward the temple and thanked the lord for keeping his daughter safe. He prayed. Prayed and promised the lord a new golden gateway to his abode.

Thirty minutes later, Stanley peeped his head into the small opening made in the wall and asked for a tool to break down the barrier from the other side. "Make sure you strike at the joints. Don't break the stone. We can put them back together later." he instructed before pulling back into the enclosure.

A while later, Swamy was able to pull his daughter out from the widened opening in the wall. A shivering Tharani embraced her father with tears in her reddened eyes. She barely smiled at her father before fainting in his arms. Tharani's clothes were damp and cold, and her body warm.

"You have to take her home quickly!" Stanley spoke before he came out entirely through the hole in the wall. "She has a fever." Stanley himself did not look well. Mud-stained clothes and bruised arms. Swamy wondered at how pale a white man could look. He picked up Tarani in his arms and instructed Nagabhushanam to take Stanley home and attend to him.

Stanley frowned, seeing Tharani. Not knowing how long they would have to wait and with limited fuel, the fire had to be kept at a bare minimum. It was not until a long time later that Stanley saw Tharani shivering violently, lying on the cold stone floor. He managed to rub some heat into her hands. But she would not let him touch her feet. He had built a fire with whatever coconut husk, shell, and flowers were around. He realized he had fallen asleep when he was startled by the clank of metal and the muffled voices.

Tharani's hand was still in his. He had carried her closer to the wall and tried waking her up by repeatedly calling her name. For that was all he knew. Seeing her now limp in her father's arms disturbed Stanley. It was odd the way he was feeling. He had sensed the way the girl had fought to stay awake and alert despite what she felt until she could hold on no longer. They had barely spoken to each other in the past two days, and he had felt a strong sense of protectiveness and helplessness when he held her in his arms. Stanley shook his head. It is the fever, of course. "Will she be alright?" he asked.

Swamy nodded. "Take care, Stanley garu. Nagabhushanam will take you home. I...I am quite grateful to you for saving her life. I have to hurry now."

They nodded at each other, and Swamy rushed out of place. Swamy carried his daughter towards the waiting cart with a heart filled with relief and a prayer to the lord on his lips.

True to the world around him, the whispers reached his ears before he even lay down his daughter in the bullock cart.

"*They were alone..*"

"*...in there*"

"*A white man...*"

"*...did you see their clothes...*"

"*....who will marry...*"

The whispers grew louder.

5

*"I hope you understand my position
Swamy,"* Venkataiah said.
Swamy did not respond. Barely had he had the time
to breathe a sigh of relief at finding his daughter
alive, and the whole village began to whisper about
the company in which she was found. The rumors had
reached home before they did. He was not naive to
think that they would not be any consequences. The
marriages had been postponed in light of the events
that took place. Swamy had personally visited
Prabhavathi's in-laws to explain the situation. The
couple had gracefully agreed to wait for the right
time. What he did not think of doing was to request
his own sister and brother-in-law. Given the
proximity of their relationship, Swamy thought his
brother-in-law would understand his predicament. It
angered him, now, to know that that was not the case.
*"Do you not trust Tharani, Bawagaru? Or is it my
upbringing that you question?"* he asked through
clenched teeth.

"It is the world that I do not trust, Swamy. I will not have people pointing at my family or questioning my family name," Venkataiah sighed. *"Swamy...I have nothing against Tharani. She is like my daughter, but you cannot deny that she brought this fate upon herself."*

"Your son took them there!"

"On their insistence!"

Before Swamy could respond in anger, Gowri Devi intervened. With folded hands, she approached her brother-by-marriage *"Annaya garu.."* she pleaded, *"The whole village has been informed of the marriage. If you break the engagement at this time, what will happen to my daughter..what will people say about her. My husband will lose the honor he has had for so many years. Please...I beg of you. I have complete faith in my daughter. She is not that kind of person..please Annaya!"*

"Gowri..." Swamy stopped his pleading wife.

"What about my father's honor, sister?" questioned Venkataiah. *"He is still alive, and I cannot allow the whispers from this house to disgrace the last years of his life."*

Swamy shut his eyes and took a deep breath. *"What does Nagabhushanam say?"*

Venkataiah tilted his chin up. *"He will do what is needed to protect his family name and honor."*

Swamy stopped his wife from responding and indicated that she leave the room. *"Be with the girls,"* He said softly. With tears in her eyes and a hand to her mouth, Gowri Devi left the room. Swamy turned to his brother-in-law. *"I do not think there is anything else to be discussed,"* he stated.

"Swamy.." Venkataiah tried to pacify.

Swamy raised his hand. *"I am sure you will understand if I do not want to talk about this any further,"* He asked his young son, Varaha Swamy, to show his uncle the way out of the house. As upset as he was by what his parents were going through, the boy reluctantly followed his father's orders. A miffed Venkataiah stomped out of the house.

Swamy found the three ladies huddled on the bed crying when he walked into his daughter's room. Seeing her father, Tharani ran and fell at his feet. *"I am so sorry, Naana! Please forgive me! I did not do anything wrong! I just wanted to see the lord. I would not do anything that would bring dishonor to the family! Please believe me!"*

Swamy gently pulled his daughter up and wiped her tears. *"Why ask for forgiveness when you have not done anything wrong."* He smiled despite the sadness in his heart. *"I have faith in my children."* He walked her over to the bed and sat her down. He took Prabhavathi's hand and held both his daughters' hands in his. *"I want you both to understand this. What happened has happened. We cannot change that. We cannot stop people from talking about it. Even if they do not say anything in front of us, they will do it behind us."* He took a deep breath. It was not easy for him to look at their saddened faces. His family was everything to him. Yes, what happened was very unfortunate. He still had to come to terms with that.

"There are consequences for what happened, and there might be more to come."

"Forgive me, Naana! Please forgive me! I have failed you as a daughter!" Tharani sobbed.

"No, Ranamma. I will have failed as a father if I give into the rumors of the world." he ran his hand over her head. Swamy did not believe in sacrificing his present and future for a dead past. He had fought once to get his daughters married, but the world did not relent. Every attempt to find one man, even among his family and friends, who valued virtue over superstition and horoscope, failed and disappointed him. He resolved to have faith in god than in man. But what had his god done?! Swamy closed his eyes shut and begged for forgiveness. How can he pledge his life to god for saving his child one day and then curse him the next day for what people were saying?!

"I will do whatever I can..." he said in a steady voice, *"to get us out of this situation. I want you girls to be brave. These are small things. You should not allow them to question you. Did you understand? Can you do that for Naana?"* The girls nodded. Swamy then turned to his wife and embraced her. His friend. Married at the young age of ten, Gowri Devi grew up in this very house. They played together, grew up together, and fell in love. Swamy could not claim to have a friend dearer than his wife, and he knew that the family was what she cherished the most. They had

braved tough times before, and they would do it again. They raised good girls and will not let the world taint their children. *"Everything will be alright, Amulu,"* he addressed his wife with a name only he called her. *"We need to have faith in ourselves and god. If he brought this upon us, he will save us from it."*

Gowri Devi nodded. *"Do you think Pra.."*

Swamy raised a finger to his wife's lips. *"Let us go down"* He turned to his daughters and comforted them again before walking out of the room with his wife. *"I have not heard anything from Prabhavathi's in-laws as yet. But..."* he squeezed his wife's hand gently..*"We should be prepared for any consequences. When our family has been the cause of this situation, we cannot expect....."*

Swamy's son came running up the stairs. *"Naana, akka's father-in-law, came. He is waiting for you."*

Gowri Devi looked at her husband with dismal hope.

Swamy sighed. *"Well, better sooner than later."*

Swamy greeted his friend and to-be-relative with folded hands. He almost did not want this conversation, knowing how it might end. But, he would rather face it than postpone the inevitable. *"Please sit down. I hope it was not a very tiring journey for you."*

Thirupathi Rao, Prabhavathi's soon-to-be father-in-law, was a tall man with a brooding face, unlike his son, who had a very welcoming smile. The son, obviously, took after his mother in his fair looks and

social nature. After the greetings, Thirupathi Rao waited for Varaha Swamy to be signaled to leave the room. *"I will not beat around the bush Swamy garu."* His deep, baritone voice resonated in the room. Thirupathi Rao cleared his throat and continued in a softer voice," *I was very happy, fortunate in fact when our alliance came through."* he paused and looked straight at Swamy's face. Swamy straightened his shoulders and braced himself. He knew what was coming. Thirupathi Rao continued, *"The rumors of the white man and your daughter have made their way to our town. I am sure you understand that those rumors will affect the impending marriage given that it does not show your family in a good light."*
Swamy sneered, *"My brother-in-law was here this morning* Thirupathi Rao *garu. I am not going to hide things from you. He has broken his son's engagement with my younger daughter."*
"Venkataiah came to my home a week ago, Swamy," Thirupathi Rao spoke, almost embarrassed to confess, *"He told me that he intended to break the engagement."*
Anger flared in Swamy's chest. Balling his fists at his sides, he stood up from his chair and walked away from the man to control his emotions. He prayed to Shiva to give him the strength to hold himself together. Taking a deep breath, he faced Thirupathi Rao. *"Am I to assume that you too..."*
"I am here to discuss how this matter can be rectified," Thirupathi Rao stated flatly.

Swamy frowned. *"What do you mean?"* he asked, wondering if there was hope to his humiliation.

"Swamy garu, not being able to find a suitable girl for my son had been my only failure until we met your family. I will not have that destroyed by what society has to say about an unfortunate situation that nobody had control of. I respect you, Swamy garu, and I don't intend to break our relationship. So, if there is anything that can be done to salvage this situation, we should do it." he stated.

Anger steamed away, and tears welled up in Swamy's eyes. This was not expected. He batted his eyelids to keep tears from flowing down. *"My brother-in-law made it quite clear that he does not...."*

"It is the white man I am talking about."

"I do not understand?" Swamy indeed did not.

"Venkataiah made it quite clear to us, too, that he did not wish to go forward with your alliance," Thirupathi Rao said, omitting the part where Venkataiah tried to convince Thirupathi Rao, too, from going ahead with their alliance. That detail was not necessary for Swamy to know. *"So, I think we need to address the source of the problem."*

"Stanley garu?" Swamy had been so immersed in what was happening around him that he had not given thought to Stanley after Swamy was ensured that their family physician was attending to Stanley's injuries and health. A few days ago, the physician had informed him that Stanley was a robust man who did not take well to spending time in the bed or his room

longer than necessary. He was already up and about the excavation site clearing up the mud and rocks. Though Swamy understood what Thirupathi Rao was suggesting, he did not see it as a viable solution. The man was from a different world, a different culture, a different religion. Their way of life was so utterly different that the thought of an alliance between their families was not natural or imaginable.

"Is that how it is said?" Thirupathi Rao smiled. *"I could not twist my tongue enough to pronounce his name. I wrote it down on a piece of paper and showed it"*

"Showed his name? I cannot understand what you are saying, Thirupathi Rao *garu?"*

"I have a thurky friend in the Nizam's ministry." Thirupathi Rao explained, *"Stunle garu was commissioned by my friend to dig up an old property of the Nizam. They had to inquire about him before making him part of the contract."*

"And?"

"He is a wealthy man, Swamy garu. His father was the..the...I forgot what my friend said..but it meant to say that he was the zamindar of his village and owned a lot of property. Their family name has generations of history and wealth in that land.... and being the oldest son, Stunle is the heir to all that wealth."

"Then why is he roaming around here digging for wealth?" Swamy asked.

Chalapathi Rao laughed. *"People are known to have weird passions, Swamy garu. I can only guess that he enjoys doing it. You know how boys are these days. They are restless and strive to do things out of the norm. I am sure he will settle down in a couple of years."*

Swamy contemplated Thirupathi Rao's disclosure. Is this man actually suggesting what Swamy thinks he is offering? *"You are asking me to...."*

"Unknowingly, as it might have happened, your daughter and the white man came together in the presence of god. I do not doubt your daughter's integrity, Swamy garu. All I am saying is that instead of seeing the situation as a misfortune, look at it as divine intervention. The man is from a respected and well-to-do family." Thirupathi Rao raised his hand to stall Swamy from speaking, *"My son's marriage depends on your daughter's wedding, Swamy garu. I cannot go ahead with this alliance with a scandal attached to its name."*

"I cannot do that! We are worlds apart. Tharani..." Chalapathi Rao's brooding gaze deepened as he looked Swamy straight in the eye and questioned him, *"Will you sacrifice your daughters' lives for honor, Swamy?"*

6

Stanley smiled at the paper in his hand. This was the
news he had been waiting for six months. The Society
of Antiquaries of London scheduled his presentation
for their next annual meeting. This was good news.
He was unsure if they would accept his work, given
that it was from India. Now, he was sure they would
be surprised, if not excited, at his presentation of the
Nizam's treasure tunnel and Swamy's temple
complex. There was work to be done. He will have to
write to Nizam for permission and request the tunnel
painting that was not completed till after he left for
his current assignment. He would also need an artist
to draw essential pictures of the Temple complex.
He folded the letter and was about to place it in his
pocket when he noticed a worker carrying a
precariously tilted rubble-filled basket on his head.
"Careful!" Stanley grabbed the man from slipping
backward. "*Jag..jag..jagtha*?" Stanley tried to
pronounce the Telugu word he had often heard
Nagabhushanam use when telling people to be

careful. The man merely smiled at Stanley and went about his work.

The first thing Stanley needed to do was to get the temple all sorted and cleaned up. He looked around. Most of the last two weeks were spent clearing the rocks and boulders. The men were now washing out the stone pillars and removing the water. The ground around the dugout temple area was ramped down with small stone pillars lining the periphery.

A temple architect was summoned to begin work on building the temple's outer gates and steps leading to the temple. Stanley had immensely enjoyed the talk with the architect. The entire science of temple architecture was fascinating. His excavations of the smaller temples and oddly placed lone pillars made sense to him now. With the architect happy to share information about the different styles of temple designs and their significance to science, astrology, history, and geography Stanley thought it would be a fascinating addition to his presentation.

Moving up the ramp, he noticed Swamy standing atop the dugout and waved the letter at him. Swamy walked down and laid a hand on Stanley's shoulder. "How are you feeling, Stanley garu?" he asked respectfully. Stanley had seen Swamy address everybody. "I could not come to see you after that day. We had a few problems at home," Swamy continued apologetically.

Stanley frowned. "Is she alright?"

"Yes, she is. It took some time. She is fine now."

"I would not be surprised if she fought it through," Stanley remembered how Tharani was practical enough to accept her situation and do what was required at that moment. A quality he, in retrospect, respected.

Swamy smiled at the compliment. It was not often a man acknowledged the spirit of a woman. Noticing the letter in Stanley's hand, he enquired, "Is that a letter from your family? You look delighted."

"This?" Stanley handed the letter to Swamy. "No. No." He grinned. "Not from my family. From The Society of Antiquaries of London. The one that I told you about three months ago. They have accepted my submission and want me to discuss my discoveries in their next annual meet."

"Ah. You will be talking about this temple?"

"Yes. And also about the treasure tunnel, we dug for the Nizam."

"Oh. Good. Good. Let me know if you need any help" He directed Stanley towards the seating area under a banyan tree."Stanley garu.." Swamy spoke after a pause, "You have been working with us for eight months, and I still do not know anything about your family."

"My family?" Stanley asked, puzzled.

Swamy sat down on the chair and indicated the same to Stanley. "Yes. When will I have the honor of meeting your father? I would like to invite your family here."

Stanley laughed. "No offense, Mr.Swamy.
Unfortunately, my mother does not have...well...does
not take well to warm weather."
"Your father?"
"My father passed away a few years ago."
"Hmm." Swamy looked at his hands. How was he to
do this? Was he doing the right thing? Help me, god!!
Swamy prayed.
"What is the matter, Mr.Swamy?" Stanley noted the
hesitation in Swamy. He had not known the older
man to hold back. Despite his limited ability to speak
English, Swamy had spoken to him directly since the
first time they met and had improved much more.
"What is bothering you?"
Swamy raised his head and looked Stanley in the
face. If this is god's will, then so be it. "Stanley
garu.." he spoke with a calmness that masked the
apprehension his heart felt. He cleared his throat and
continued, "Nagabhushanam's father has canceled his
son's wedding with my daughter."
Stanley frowned. "With Tarani?"
Swamy nodded.
"Why?" As he asked the question, Stanley had an odd
feeling that he knew the answer. And he did not like
it.
It was not easy for Swamy to answer the question. He
needed to articulate it well so as not to offend
Stanley. He cannot blame the young man for trying to
save his daughter. "His father did not want the
marriage to take place. Nagabhushanam is just

obeying his father," He finished, hoping that Stanley would read between the lines and understand what Swamy was trying to say.

"What?!" Stanley had hoped for a different answer. He looked at Swamy and wondered why he had hesitated to tell him this. Swamy did not need to say to him about his private affairs. But he did. And he hesitated to do so. "Was it because of what happened at the temple?" He asked.

Swamy glanced away from Stanley and nodded in confirmation.

Stanley did not know what to say. He should not have been surprised at the outcome of that event. Any girl would have met with the same fate even in England. It would have been a scandal that rang through the ballrooms and cardrooms season after season. Apparently, a different land did not have a different perspective on what could have, in reality, been a tragic situation. "Mr.Swamy.." Stanley spoke firmly. Nothing wrong happened, and it was unfair that the girl had to be punished for it. "I assure you, nothing happened between your daughter and me to warrant this kind of outcome," he said. "I will speak to Nagabhushanam. I am sure he will understand."

Swamy smirked. "The decision is not in his hands Stanley garu." Swamy had hoped that Nagabhushanam would come around to meet him and at least tell Swamy that he tried to speak to his father. But there was no word from him or of him. The day Tharani was rescued from the temple was the last

Swamy had seen or heard from his nephew. Swamy was sure Nagabhushanam loved his daughter, but his love was not strong enough to override his father's tainted views. "His father does not want his family to get a bad name Stanley garu. And...and" Swamy swallowed. It was tough enough to explain the situation. He cleared his throat. "Life as a woman, in our culture, is not the same as it is for men, Stanley garu. A woman's virtue is weighed by the purity of her body and not her soul" His eyes are misted. "I fought against society for cursing my daughters with a fate they have no control over. I searched for a man who would marry Prabhavathi for the woman she is and not for the star she was born under. I even offered my wealth Stanley garu" Swamy shook his head in disappointment and sighed, "But...people value astrology more than good sense." Swamy raised his *kanduva* and dabbed his forehead. "Prabhavathi's father-in-law wishes to go ahead with the wedding Stanley garu..but only if.." Swamy looked visibly agitated.

This is the first time Stanley has seen Swamy frowning "only if what, Mr.Swamy?" He asked "Only if...Tharani is married at the same time" Swamy forced himself to look at Stanley. In his heart, he knew that Stanley was innocent. Being from a foreign land and not having any idea of the culture of this land, Stanley had been respectful to every person he met. Stanley was a learned man, and Swamy had always enjoyed his interaction with this *Sahib* with the golden hand. Stanley's manner of speech and behavior testified to his good upbringing. And that was the only reason Swamy had even thought seriously about this marriage prospect. Looking at Stanley now, Swamy felt a tinge of guilt. What had happened was not Stanley's fault. Still, Swamy had promised his family that he would do whatever it took to rectify this situation. Swamy stood up and held his hands together in a *namaste*. "Stanley garu...as a father of two daughters whose lives have become a puppet in the hands of society, I can only request you...I know," he hesitated. "I know you are not responsible...but...I can only appeal to the honorable man that you are... I can only request..."

Stanley frowned, knowing what was coming.

"Mr.Swamy I.."

"Marry my daughter Stanley garu" Swamy bowed his head. "Marry Tharani."

7

"Tharani, please stop crying. You will fall sick if you continue like this. My sweet sister, na. Eat this." Prabhavathi pleaded, *"You haven't eaten anything for two days, and your face is beginning to look like Nana's old aunt."* She quipped, trying to bring some humor into the sad situation.

But Tharani would not stop. She could not stop. Nagabhushanam's words haunted her mind. The same conversation had stung her heart and made her numb till she reached home to find out that her father had asked the English man to marry her.

The dam of emotions broke down, and Tharani became inconsolable.

From childhood, she had envisioned Nagabhushanam as her husband and loved him. Even when she was made aware that she might not get married till Prabhavathi did, Tharani had not given up hope on Nagabhushabam. She believed very strongly that she would marry him one day. She knew Nagabhushanam felt the same for her. That was the only reason she had approached him that evening.

Knowing Nagabhushanam's routine of visiting his maternal uncle every two weeks, Tharani had begged her 15-year-old brother, Varaha Swamy, to take her to personally talk with Nagabhushanam. She was sure Nagabhushanam would change his decision after seeing and talking to her. But what played out was completely different from what she had envisioned. *"You should not have come, Tharani,"* were his first words. There was no smile on his face. No relief on having seen her standing healthy in front of him. In the few seconds, before he turned away, Tharani searched his eyes for any hint of affection. She knew he was not happy. She could make that out.

"Why are you behaving like that, Bawa?" Why won't you look at me?" Tears began to roll down Tharani's face. *"please don't do this."* she pleaded.*" I will talk to Mamaiah. I will try to convince him. Please, Bawa! Don't you trust me? Talk to the white man if you want. He will tell you. He will tell you that I am innocent."*

"Tharani, please don't talk like that."

Nagabhushanam spoke with misted eyes, *"I do not need a white man to tell me what kind of girl you are."*

Tharani smiled through her tears. *"So you don't believe what the people are saying,"* she said more to herself.

"No. I don't." Nagabhushanam replied.

"Then you will talk to Mamaiah about our marriage?" a hope flared within her heart.

Nagabhushanam swallowed hard. The hurt and pain he felt when his father declared that the marriage would not happen were still raw. His throat had ached after his argument with his father. It was exhausting to restrain his emotions against a father who had always told people what to do without considering their opinions or efforts. Unable to rationalize with his son, he finally declared that if Nagabhushanam married Tharani, he would have to be ready to light his father's funeral pyre the same day. From there, it took little effort for an angry father and a crying mother to break their obedient son's will to marry the girl he had loved since childhood. *"My father won't agree, Tharani,"* Nagabhushanam replied firmly. He prayed that Tharani would understand the unspoken emotion and go away. He knew she would be angry. But she surprised him.

Tharani walked over to him and held his hands. *"That is ok, Bawa. I understand why Mamaiah would be angry. But.. But... You trust me, right? That is enough for me."* The hopeful look in Tharani's eyes bled his heart. And so did the following words. *"Let's run away Bawa. We will run away and get married. Nana will be a little angry initially, but he will accept it. He will understand. "* She shook her head, *"Mamaiah may be angry too. But with time, I am sure he will accept us too."*

Nagabushnam slowly moved Tharani's hand off him. *"It might be easy for you, Tharani.."* he spoke in a steady voice, *"but I am not going to disgrace my father. Forgive me. I cannot...."* he swallowed hard. His father's warning rang in his head *"Your mother will become a widow, and you will be the reason for it!!".* Nagabushnam looked away from Tharani. He could not look her in the eye and lie, *"I cannot marry you, Tharani. I will not bring disgrace... Tharani, please leave,"* he pleaded. He did not know how long he could hold back the pain.

Tharani would not give up. *"Look at me, Bawa."* she requested. "Please look at me and say that you will not marry me."

Nagabushnam did not turn around. *"Looking at you will not change my decision Tharani. It is for your good that I am telling you. Don't ever come to see me again."* he did not wait for a reply and walked away. A shocked Tharani stood rooted to the ground, paralyzed of thought and movement. She did not know what to make of Nagabushnam's statement. How could he tell her to not meet him again? Did he not know that she loved him? Did he not love her? The tears stopped flowing, and her brother's call receded into the background. She was numb as Varaha pulled her away and sat her gently in the bullock cart. She did not know when she reached home or how she went into her room. She was jarred into reality by her father's announcement about her marriage to Stanley.

"Kill me, nana!" she pleaded. *"It is better you kill me than get married to that white man!"* Tharani cried.

Anger flashed across Swamy's face. The thought that his daughter chose death over fighting a difficult situation saddened him. *"Why is it so easy for you to speak of death, Ranamma?"* he questioned in a strained voice. *"Do you know how it feels to lose a child? Your mother..."* he pointed at his crying wife, *"Your mother did not eat a grain of rice or sleep a wink in the two days we were trying to dig you out. Everybody told us you were dead. But your mother prayed. She never left the temple afraid... Afraid that God would take her silence for acceptance of your death!"* Swamy grabbed Tharani by her arms. *" Do you know how it feels to lose your child?! The very child that I fought the society for and I continue to fight and protect against the fickleness of this society?"* tears filled his eyes. *"Do you know how it feels to imagine the child you raised and loved laying dead under the rubble of rocks? I prayed, Ranamma... For you! All I asked the lord was to keep my daughter alive. I held on even when it looked bleak. How dare you make light of the love and respect your mother and I have raised you with?! "* He straightened his back. *"I have always believed that I raised my children as strong individuals who can face and overcome any tough situation. But... I am forced to believe I am wrong. If you find it easier to face death than the future God has willed for you, then the only thing to do, Ranamma,"* a teary-eyed Swamy cupped his daughter's face with his hands, *"I cannot bear the*

*thought of losing you...or any my children. If you
have to die... So will I."*
"No... No... No, Nana," Tharani shook her head
vigorously. *"Please forgive me. Please forgive me. I...
I... I don't know what to do, Nana. How can I marry a
white man?! I... I don't know anything about him or
how they live? I don't know what to speak. How will I
live, Nana?!*
Swamy embraced his daughter. *"Everybody is the
child of the same God, Ranamma. You will treat them
and their culture with the same respect you treat
ours."* He kissed her forehead.

At the other end of the village, in the house that
Swamy had provided for Stanley, Mrs.Potter was
feeling emotional and helpless at what was
happening. "I will not have you do this to yourself,
master Stanley!" She shook her cherubic face quite
emphatically. "You be sure I will write to my lady
about this!"
"Won't it be too late by that time, Mrs.Potter? "
Stanley twirled the wine in his glass. The light from
the oil lamp made the dark liquid light up into
burgundy. "Even if my mother went into a fit and
would not allow the messenger to leave, it will be a
good six months since your letter to her and her angry
reply." He pointed out in a non emotional tone.
"How can you be calm about this, master Stanley?
You cannot allow these people to treat you like this! I

do not understand why you have to be the one to be sacrificed at the altar?!"

Stanley laughed. His first since Swamy's request. Poor Mrs.Potter was turning herself red with anger over what was asked of her master and what her master had decided to do about it. Stanley stood and towered his six-foot frame over his former nanny turned cook. "Look at me, Mrs.Potter. Do you really think that these people are forcing me into a marriage?"

"I think that they are taking advantage of your kind nature Mr.Stanley." the portly lady could not help but cool down at that charming smile. "This sort of thing would just not happen in our country, is all I am saying. They have cornered a lonely man. "

Stanley poured wine into a glass and handed it to the old lady. Mrs. Potter had been his childhood friend. The cook made special treats for her favorite little master. Having retired from work after all her children were well settled in service jobs, Mrs. Potter was a content grandmother until her husband passed away. Then, she took up Stanley's offer to accompany him to India. Having never stepped out of England, it was a bold step for her. But how. Could she ever refuse the adorable Master Stanley? It did not matter that the once chubby, rosy-cheeked boy was now a strapping young man. " Ooh, master Stanley!" she spoke worriedly. "You don't have to marry that girl to save her honor?"

"Then how do you suggest I do it, Mrs. Potter?"

"YOU don't have to marry her, is what I am saying," Mrs. Potter emphasized.

Stanley smiled. "You seem to forget that it was with me that she was found in that temple."

"That is not the reason for marrying someone!!!" an exasperated Mrs. Potter exclaimed.

"If this was England, I would have been called out by the girl's father for a duel, Mrs. Potter."

"But this is not England, Master Stanley!!"

"The value we attribute to a girl's virtue does not change with the country Mrs. Potter."

"Master Stanley..."

"Mrs. Potter.." Stanley spoke with a calmness that the elder cook knew far too well. Stanley smiled a little "Don't get too worked up, nanny. I have not told Swamy that I will marry his daughter."

"But you have decided!" Mrs. Potter exclaimed.

"I have not made a decision yet."

"I have known you since you were born, Master Stanley. I know that look, and I know that demeanor. You have decided, and I see that."

Stanley laughed. "She is not all that bad, Mrs. Potter." Tharani wasn't. Her doe eyes were a sight that Stanley could never forget. Thickly lined with the black liquid that Stanley had so often seen with Indian women, Tharani's eyes were the first thing he noticed about her. "Though I wonder if I will ever get her name right. Ta... Thru... Truni?"

"Oh lord, have mercy on me!" Mrs. Potter exclaimed, "Master Stanley, you cannot treat the matter of marriage so lightly. You are not buying peanuts, for Christ's sake!!"

Stanley's urge to laugh at Mrs. Potter's cries got diverted by a knock at the door. He smiled. "That must be Sir Cullingham."

8

What do you mean I will not be given credit for it"
Stanley frowned at the news that Sir Cullingham had
just delivered to him.

The older gentleman pulled out his monocle and
cleaned it. "It means exactly what I have said. You
will not be given any drawings or credit for
excavating the tunnels you spent an entire year
digging out."

"How can he do that? That was the deal he had agreed
upon before we even started work. And he reassured
me of the same when I was leaving Hyderabad. How
can he go against his own words."

"Well, I would not say the Nizam went against his
word. I am sure he is not even aware of this
development, " the somber reply.

"What do you mean?"

"It was the Nizam's minister who has asked me, or
should I say, told me, to relay the message that you
are as good as nonexistent to them unless.."

"Unless?"

"Unless you got married.."

"What in god's name does my marriage have to do with this?!!" Stanley burst out. The conversation was getting confusing with every sentence.

"Oh, the whole point is about your marriage, Stanley."

"Sir Cullingham, I appreciate you coming to give me this news. But, I am afraid your objective is not being met. I am unable to understand what it is that you are trying to tell me."

Sir Cullingham sighed and took a deep puff from his pipe that Stanley lighted for him. "Your prospective father-in-law is apparently a very dear friend of the Nizam's minister, Stanley. It is upon his wish that the papers will be withheld from you...Until and unless you marry his daughter."

Stanley was confused. Much as he was angry at being denied what was truly his credit, he was not very sure of Swamy's involvement in this matter. Swamy, Stanley knew, was not the kind of person to impose on anybody. But..then..he was a human and the father who, for whatever reasons, was finding it very hard to marry off his daughters. Having been considered a prime catch in London, Stanley was quite aware of the lengths people went to get their daughters married. Very glaring evidence was open for everybody to see year after year during the 'London Season. But would Swamy stoop to such a level? Could he coerce a man into marrying his daughter?

Stanley understood why he was the reason Tharani's marriage was broken, but it was not his fault. And why did Swamy not wait for Stanley's answer before doing something like this? "Why would Mr.Swamy do something like this." He thought out aloud.

"So, it is true?" Sir Cullingham exclaimed.

"What is true?"

"That you are marrying the Indian girl."

"No." Stanley shook his head. "I mean, I have not made up my mind..."

"But you have not refused?"

"It is a little complicated. You probably would understand if you knew the whole of it. Mr. Swamy did ask me to marry his daughter. But, It was not out of his own free will. Neither was I his first choice."

Sir Cullingham leaned back in his chair. "I have all the time, Stanley. Please do elaborate. Maybe we can find a solution to this predicament. Before that, could you ask your cook to send in some refreshments? It was a long, dusty ride over here. I must admit, I am pretty desperate for my boarding orders back to London. I cannot tolerate the heat anymore. Can you believe I wake up soaking wet? It is no wonder these Indians do not wear as many clothes! "

Over the course of some freshly made English snacks, Sir Cullingham was upraised off the events that led to Stanley's current stance as a groom.

" Hmm." The older gentleman slid a finger across his blonde handlebar mustache. "And why is this a matter of such grave thought, Stanley?"

Stanley knew Sir Cullingham possessed a somewhat superfluous personality, but that he would not see a pronounced disparity in the situation made him wonder what the older man was thinking. He raised his brows in a nonverbal question.

"Come, come, boy. Don't be so naive." when Stanley did not respond to his slight jibe, the senior gentleman sighed and continued to explain, "Well, you don't have to live with the women you marry."

Stanley was not surprised at the suggestion made, given the reputation of the person who made it. But that he would suggest something like that or that he saw Stanley the same as himself irked him. Stanley was not a social recluse nor a man of ill repute. He had never played with the emotions of the fairer sex and was not about to start now. "Are you suggesting that I not honor the marriage Sir Cullingham?" he spoke with restrained anger.

"By all means, do, my dear boy. By all means, do. If...your intent is to marry that girl. But if the reason is anything other than love, I suggest you do it to your advantage. You do not have to abide by something you do not believe in."

"So, you suggest I marry her for the papers and leave her."

Sir Cullingham shook his head in denial. "No. No. Of course not. Marry her. Enjoy the exotic beauty. Get the papers. Sail back to England and stay true to your native land. With the girl's father's wealth, you need not have to worry about abandoning her."

Stanley tightened his grip on the wine glass "Sir Cullingham..." he spoke in a measured tone, "I am thankful to you for upraising me of the events. I really do appreciate you having come all this way to do that. What I do not understand is your insistence on suggesting indecent proposals."

"It is not indecent, Stanley. It is what these people deserve for the unchristian way of their lives. Do you see the way these women dress? We have whores who dress more decently than these bare-chested women. It is absolutely hideous."

"Gratitude has never been one of your virtues, Sir Cullingham."

"What do you mean?"

Stanley sneered, "You have made more money in this land than you could have ever done in your own country, Sir." Stanley made an undeniable reference to Sir Cullingham's financial reputation in England. The man had sold the last bit of his self-depleted family fortune to buy a ticket to India. "The people here have always greeted us with the utmost courtesy and respect. Yet, you choose to slight their women in a manner that does not speak much about your own."

A miffed Cullingham stood from his chair. "It would have served you right to have not informed you. I bring you news of your impending doom, and you dare to mock me, Stanley?!"

"Trust me, Sir, when I tell you that the news you gave me would not have changed the course of my life in any manner."

9

Gowri Devi watched as her husband walked in through the door and handed him a small tumbler of water to wash his feet.

Swamy sat down in a chair and reached for the glass of water that Prabhavathi held out for him. He looked at his wife.

Gowri Devi was wringing her fingers in nervousness. *"What did he say?"* she asked in haste just as her husband had opened his mouth to speak.

Swamy smiled half-heartedly. *"He agreed.."*

Gowri cleared her brow and smiled in relief. After sending out a quick and quiet prayer to her Lord, she noticed that there was more her husband wanted to say. *"What happened? Are you not happy?"*

"I am happier than I look like Gowri.."

"But?"

Swamy leaned back in the easy chair. *"There was something in the way Stanley spoke to me."*

"Was he rude to you?"

Swamy shook his head. *"No. No. He has always been a well-spoken man. But It... It felt like he was restraining himself from saying something."*
"Do you think he wants dowry?"
Swamy laughed at his wife's question. *"I don't think he even knows what that means. No. No. He did not ask for any such thing. But.."*
"But?"
"He is a little reluctant to follow our traditions and marriage rituals. And I can understand that."
"But how can he marry without marriage rituals? What does he want to do?"
"Don't be silly, Gowri. You cannot expect him to follow our rituals without knowing what they mean. Would you follow theirs?" Swamy sighed and rubbed his forehead with his fingers. *"He asked me if he should get a ring made for Tarani. I told him that we do not exchange rings but that he has to tie the Thaali around Tharani's neck. He agreed. But.."*
"But?"
"He will not sit down or go through all the rituals. He said he would tie the thali in our presence but nothing more. Tharani will have to leave immediately for his house."
"How can he say something like that..." Gowri spoke anxiously.
Swamy raised his hand to stall her outburst. He pulled the chair beside him closer and directed Gowri to sit in it. Gowri shook her head. She was feeling way too agitated to sit down. Swamy held her hand and gently

pulled her close. He reassuringly squeezed her hand.
"You have to understand, Gowri. For whatever reason God chose to put us through this situation, it is not normal to him and us. As apprehensive as you are about giving our child to him, don't you think he must be equally apprehensive about marrying her?"
Swamy put a finger to Gowri's lips when she started to speak. *" Stanley comes from a family that has a good standing in their society, similar to ours in our society. He does not have to go through this marriage. "*
"But Tharani's wedding was broken because she was seen with him!" Gowri stated, teary-eyed.
"That is wrong, Gowri." Swamy sighed. *"Trying to save our daughter should not be held against him. He did not have to marry our daughter, yet he agreed to do so. He understood our plight. Being an outsider, he understood the pain our people have inflicted upon us. Stanley is an honorable man Gowri. What he asks of us is very little compared to what we have asked of him."* Swamy stood and ambled away from Gowri. Turning around, he thought aloud. *" I just have to find a way to convince Prabhavathi's father-in-law."*
His anxious wife sprang to her feet. *"Speak to him about what? What did he say?"*
"Calm down. It is nothing out of the ordinary. Prabhavathi's father-in-law asked to have Tharnamma married in the morning, before Prabhavathi, just to ensure that Stanley stood true to his word. He called it a suggestion." Swamy sneered

slightly. *"But he more or less implied that I should do it."* Swamy took a deep breath.

"But Stanley garu did not agree?" Gowri asked meekly, almost dreading the answer.

"That is the part that is puzzling me" Swamy rubbed his forehead with his fingers. *"He agreed to the marriage, asked me if he needs to buy or do anything from his side, and agreed to tie the thaali instead of exchanging rings. Even asked me what Ranamma needed to get his house ready for her. But..."*

"But?"

"He refused to get married in the morning. He said that he did not want a crowd. Family, he was okay with. But nobody else. I tried telling him about the auspicious muhurtam in the morning, but he refused. He won't even be attending Prabhavathi's wedding. He said that Ranamma had to leave with him as soon as the marriage was done."

By the time Swamy was done talking, Gowri Devi had moved close to him and grasped his arm. *" I am worried. What if he does not treat our daughter well? A man who has put restrictions even before getting married, what will he do after the marriage? "* Swamy smiled gently at his wife. *"What he has asked is nothing more unusual than what most grooms' families ask. I agree it did sound a little unusual coming from him. But he is a man from another country and another culture Gowri. He probably is as scared as we are. Maybe it is his way of feeling in control of his life."*

"Maybe. Maybe. Maybe!!! Everything is a maybe."
Gowri Devi looked upwards and folded her hands in
prayer *"why have you put us in this predicament, my
lord? What are you testing us for?"* she cried, tears
rolling down her face.

Swamy hugged his wife *"Shh. The girls will hear you.
If we both start to lose out grip on our emotions, how
do you think the girls will see it?"* He wiped the tears
off her cheeks. *"Don't you trust me? I will not let
anything wrong happen to our girls. I have immense
trust in their ability to overcome any adversity they
face. We will always be with our children no matter
which part of the world. Now stop crying. You people
are my strength. You are my strength Gowri. Don't
falter now, okay?. Everything will be fine. If this is
the path God has chosen for us, we will walk it with
complete devotion and faith. And God will help us
through it. Do you understand? "*

Gowri Devi shook her head. Even though her
husband's words and faith always reassured her,
giving her daughter away to a man from an unknown
land was unsettling to a mother's heart.

The parents did not know the gamut of emotions that
arose in Tharani's heart. Standing quietly behind the
doors, Tharani heard her father talk about the white
man's refusal to oblige her father. If only she had died
that day. Her parents would have been spared the
humiliation, and she would have been spared the
heartache of her love refusing to marry her. If only
she had died that day. It was all because of that white

man. Why did he have to save her?! Why did he have to agree to this marriage?! And now, why was he not obliging her father?!

10

Stanley moved the white curtain out of the way to have a small peak out the window. The burly men, gathered under the neem tree outside his house, were now split into two groups and standing casually on either side of the main entrance gate to his home. Every few minutes, they peeked towards the house and went back to chatting with each other.

Stanley did not recognize any of the men, but he knew why they were there. And he did not like it. He doubted Swamy's role behind the Nizam's refusal to provide the documents. But, this move on Swamy's part seemed to bring him out of denial.

The door to his study opened, and Mrs. Potter walked in, dressed in a high-waisted gown. "I wondered when I would get an occasion to wear this fine dress when my daughter-in-law gifted it to me. 'You never know,' she said to me. And, here I am wearing it for your wedding Master Stanley!" she smiled at him. "Who would have thought? You getting married. That too in India! To an Indian girl!" she sat down in the chair opposite him, liberty she shared when she was alone with him. "I do not understand if I am to be happy or hysterical at your predicament?"

"Well.." Stanley said, continuing to frown at the sight outside these windows. "It is a path I chose. So, pray, Mrs. Potter. Pray, that I have made the right choice. Both for the girl and me." he looked at her and smiled.

"Oh! Master Stanley!" Mrs. Potter puffed, "Stop being so desolate! Oh, I wish you were a tiny wee lad! I would have just bundled you in my arms and carried you away from this awful moment." Stanley smiled at the too often memory of his childhood. "So when are we to leave?"

"Swamy's son is going to come to escort us to the ceremony."

"Why do we have to be escorted to the venue?" Mrs.Potter was surprised at having to be escorted to a wedding.

"That is a ritual, apparently." Stanley replied, "The bride's brother is to escort the groom to the altar, with all due respect. Swamy will be sending over some clothes for me to change into, again a ritual." he added.

"Are you going to dress like them?" Mrs. Potter sounded alarmed at the prospect of seeing Stanley dress in a *panchi*.

"No," Stanley stated.

"Did you appraise them of that?"

"No."

"Would they be offended, master Stanley?"

"It is an unusual wedding Mrs.Potter. I do not believe my dressing would alarm them quite as much as the incidents leading to these nuptials have."

"Hmm...Oh, that must be them." Mrs.Potter stood up to the knock at the door. "I will bring them over. "

"We will meet them at the door, Mrs.Potter." Stanley walked over and held out his hand to Mrs. Potter. Swamy's son, accompanied by some older men and ladies, stood at the door. He folded his hands in a *namaste* and bowed his head.

"Ah! Junior Swamy! How are you? Are you here to escort me to my wedding?" Stanley smiled.

Varaha Swamy smiled back in greeting. He turned around and took a tray, covered with velvet cloth, from a lady behind him. Extending it up to Stanley, Varaha bowed his head and said, "These are for you, Ba...Stanley garu," he spoke hesitantly.

Stanley took the tray from the boy's hand. An older lady stepped forward and handed a tray of silk garments to Mrs. Potter. Not sure what she was expected to do, Mrs. Potter accepted it with a hesitant smile. "Stanley garu has told us that you raised him as a kid. He told my father that you cared for him like his mother. This is a gift from the bride's family to the groom's family, a..." Varaha explained and paused, not sure how to address the older woman.

Mrs. Potter smiled at him " You can call me Mrs. Potter," she said. "Thank you for the lovely gift."

"Mrs.Potter." Varaha addressed, "Please, come. " he said, leading the way towards the waiting bullock carts. The carts looked very colorful and festive. Mrs.Potter was directed towards the second bullock cart, which she realized was being occupied by ladies only. Alongside the second bullock cart, a lone horse stood, not quite as festively dressed as the carriages were. "Father was not sure which you would prefer." Varaha said, "Would you be more comfortable on the horse Stanley garu?" he asked.

"I am happy I get to choose, junior Swamy." Stanley smiled.

"Please call me Varaha." the boy requested.

"I would if I knew how to pronounce your name." They both laughed. Having eased the tension, he was feeling Stanley leaned towards Varaha and asked in a whisper, "Tell me, boy. Do you know those men standing under that tree? They have been there since this morning." Stanley asked.

"Those men?" Varaha narrowed his eyes in the direction that Stanley pointed. The men, who were until now in a lazy stance, looked a little uncomfortable and began turning their backs to the marriage party. "Ballaya?" Varaha recognized one of them. "That man..in the yellow *panchi* works in our fields." he clarified. "What is he doing here? He should have been at the house?" Without another word to Stanley, Varaha called out to Ballaya, walking towards them. "*What are you doing here? Who are these men?*" Varaha asked the burly man, who bent over almost half his height, looking like a thief caught in the act.

"I... I.. I.. was told to wait here, babu. Your older sister's father-in-law asked me to escort these men and wait for further instructions. But... But we... We have not heard anything yet." he said, unsure how much to tell this young boy.

"Ok. I will tell father that you are here." Varaha said. Before he could finish what he wanted to say, Ballayya sputtered.

" Aaa... No need, babu. I am sure we are not needed anymore. I will come along." Ballayya instructed the other men to follow him.

Stanley did not wholly follow what was spoken in Telugu, but he got a jist of what transpired. Varaha Swamy obviously did not know why these men were here. And, the men were definitely here for Stanley. At least to make sure he did not escape. Stanley was not happy with the kind of distrust that Swamy was showing. He was not obliged to marry the girl. But having agreed to do so, it angered Stanley that he was being subjected to such soft bullying. First, the Nizam and now these men. He did not want to believe that Swamy would behave in such a manner, but he could not find a better explanation for what was happening. He worked himself into a quite fit by the time the marriage party reached the venue.

The Shiva temple that Stanley had helped excavate was no longer surrounded by rubble and rock. The whole perimeter of the temple was neatly laid out with stones with steps leading to the inner sanctum. Some of the newly erected pillars were decorated with flowers and mango leaves. Earthen oil lamps lined the entrance to the *garbha gudi*. Swamy and his wife were standing at the doorway when Stanley and Mrs.Potter arrived. Swamy greeted Stanley with a warm smile. "I have explained to the priest to keep the rituals as simple as possible." He said to the groom, "He will not make you do anything you are not comfortable doing." He then turned to Mrs.Potter. "I hope you will not mind me saying," he said, pointing at her shoes. "We do not cover our feet in the presence of God, as a matter of respect," he said humbly. Though a little surprised at what was asked of her to do, Mrs.Potter obliged after seeing Stanley take his shoes off while Swamy was asking her the same. Swamy's wife walked up to Stanley and greeted him by applying a dot of vermilion to his forehead. Her tight and shy smile was not reflected in her eyes. The *garbha gudi,* too, was decorated with flowers and oil lamps. The Shiva *linga* looked as if it was polished to shine in the amber glow. It was decorated with flowers and looked like a gold ornament snake wrapped around the base of the long structure. Mrs.Potter stood and watched in awe at the large *lingam. S*he could not make sense of what she saw but realized that whatever it was was to be revered.

"It is not in my power to question HIS chosen path for my daughter, Stanley garu," Swamy said, pointing at the 7-foot-tall version of Shiva. "But, words are not sufficient to convey the gratitude I feel." he folded his hands in a namaste and bowed his head. "You have saved my family's name and honor. You had agreed to hold my daughter's hand when my own left her to the mercy of society. I am. Forever. Indebted to you," he said.

Swamy's humble gesture made Stanley lose some of the steam he was built up all through the morning. He took hold of Swamy's clasped hands. What did one really say in such a situation? Stanley thought, "I can only hope that it works for the best of everybody, Mr. Swamy. I can only hope and pray. "

Swamy turned towards the *lingam.* "He brought us to this point. He will lead us further," he said solemnly. "I sure hope he does." Stanley sighed.

"Please.." Swamy said, leading Stanley to a corner of the *sanctum sanctorum,* "Once Tharani is done with her pooja, the priest will perform the marriage ceremony. You told me, in your culture, the groom gives a ring to the bride? In our culture, the groom ties a sacred thread around the bride's neck. You have to tie three knots. " Swamy picked up the *mangala sutram* from a decorated tray. "Each knot signifies a commitment. To each other. To your well-being and to your families." he explained.

A lot of questions were rising in Stanley's mind at this point. Why am I doing this? Is it fair to the girl and to me? Why did Swamy do what he did? Why this trust in me? How will this end? What have I done?. As he moved closer to where Tharani was sitting, people surrounding her moved away to clear the path.

Tharani had closed her eyes in prayer and opened them at the sudden hush of voices. She looked up only to meet Stanley's gaze. At that point, one thought ran through their minds "Are you feeling the same as me?"

11

A silence descended over the wedding party as Swamy raised his hand, signaling the musicians to stop drumming out wedding tunes.

"I do not understand Stanley garu," Swamy said. His son-in-law's sudden change in attitude threw a gloom over what was a lovely wedding ceremony. There was much less drama and tears than Swamy had anticipated. But.

"I am sorry, Mr.Swamy. But I will have to refuse your gifts."Stanley said, looking behind Swamy at the slew of bullock carts and people carrying gifts for the groom and bride. The 'gifts' were every household item needed, required, and imaginable, from gleaming silver wear and brass utensils to silk garments. Each bullock cart was filled with household items. Even a polished hardwood bed, carried by six sturdy men, was part of the procession.

"You are a very generous man, Mr.Swamy. But I cannot..."

"It is part of our tradition Stanley garu. These are from me to you and my daughter." Swamy explained.

"Your daughter is now my wife, Mr.Swamy," Stanley stated with mild authority. "I am quite capable of providing for her. Whatever you have lined up, they are things that I can afford to buy."

"I did not mean to insult you, Stanley garu!" Swamy assured, "I have never doubted your ability to look after my daughter. But..."

Stanley folded his hands in a namaste and politely tried to cut off his father-in-law's words, "It has been a long day, Mr.Swamy. If you allow me, I would like to take my bride home now."

Unsure of what he had done to make his son-in-law angry, Swamy nodded and raised his hand in a namaste. Stanley had already made it clear that he or Tharani would not be going back to Swamy's house, wherein they were expected to spend three days and nights for post-marriage rituals. With certain helplessness that he seldom felt, Swamy appealed, "Tharani has never lived away from us, Stanley garu. She... She does not know your language. She is a quick learner and a good girl." he smiled, becoming emotional. Having to let go of two daughters, at the same time, on the same day was making Swamy's heartache, especially when the future looked uncertain. He fought back the tears and continued." It is my humble request, Stanley garu. Just a little patience. She becomes stubborn when she is scared." Swamy looked towards the temple. "You and she have been destined together, by God's will. But, happiness is in your hands." he bowed his head a little

"Please forgive me if I have done anything to make you unhappy."

Stanley glanced at Tharani. His bride. She was sitting in the bullock cart, a few feet from where he was standing. She had not looked at him through most of the wedding except when he tied the sacred thread around her neck. She had raised her head to look at him when he tied the third knot. Her doe eyes, thinly lined with a black paste, something he had seen most Indian women wear, enhanced the shape of her eyes and gave her dark eyes a magnetic charm. He saw her eyes slowly brim with tears as she seemed to question him and ask him for help at the same time. At that moment, Stanley felt a stir in his heart and gut. He had a strong need to protect this girl, who was now his responsibility. His wife. He held her hand firmly as he led her around the sacred fire — seven steps for seven vows.

To Stanley's understanding, Swamy had translated the vows that the priest was chanting in Telugu.

First Vow

I promise to give my wife happiness and welfare

I, she promised, to fulfill all the duties for the household's welfare, children and family.

Second vow

I promise to protect the family and you, my wife, by all the power, in the name of God.

I promise to become your strength and remain by your side during every turbulent and tough time.

Third vow

I, your husband, promise to work for our wealth and prosperity as a couple and a noble upbringing of our kids.

Fourth vow

I, your wife, promise to nurture and maintain harmony and happiness through mutual love, respect, faith, and understanding.

Fifth vow

I accept you as my wife and my partner for life.
I promise to honor you, my husband, with love and respect.

Sixth vow

I promise to see to your welfare
I promise to be by his side, no matter what.

Seventh vow

We are now husband and wife and are one. You are mine, and I am yours for eternity.

Stanley sighed. "You told somebody would accompany my wife to our house?" he asked Swamy. Swamy hesitated. As per tradition, the bride's aunt and uncle accompanied the bride to her in-laws' house for the first couple of days. Mainly to provide the bride with a sense of comfort in an otherwise new place. Given the circumstances of this wedding, nobody from Swamy's family came forward to fulfill that aspect of the wedding. Swamy, too, did not ask. He had, instead, asked for the field man's 12-year-old son to accompany Tharani to her new home. The young boy was trained in the field and household work and knew to ride a bullock cart.

"Yes." Swamy nodded. "Juggaiah!" he called out over his shoulder. A bare-chested young boy in a knee-length dhoti hurried over, bowing down to Swamy. "He is my field man's son," Swamy said, placing his arm over the boy's shoulder. "He is very good with cows and bulls. He was born in our house. Tharani had looked after him like a younger brother. If you don't mind providing him with some shelter and food, he will be your loyal servant and a company for Ranamma." Swamy requested.

Stanley's head was feeling heavy with all the cross-talk in his mind. What he knew of Swamy and how Swamy behaved was very different from what he heard of his now father-in-law. Yet, there was evidence of an injustice that was met out to him. Despite Sir Cullingam's news, Stanley had reached out to the Nizam's minister for a copy of the tunnel promised to him. His reply was not an explicit denial of his work but an arrogant letter of the Nizam's need to deal with a disobedient subject. Anger had flared in Stanley's body, enough to smash a table. And, standing in front of him, now, was a man as humble as he had ever seen. Not wanting to delay things anymore, Stanley nodded, and, not wanting to talk any further, he walked towards Tharani.

Seeing her husband, a stranger from an unknown land, coming towards her, Tharani turned her head away. With the day's events still feeling a little muddled in his head, Stanley was not sure what he was expecting to do when he walked toward his bride.

As he approached her, a daisy tucked in the strands of her hair rolled out and began to fall. In a reflex, Stanley reached for the flower and hesitated before gently tucking it back in her hair.

Swamy sighed in relief. Small as that gesture was, what Stanley did gave Swamy a ray of hope, and he felt affirmed in his judgment of Stanley. Now, all he had to do was to find out what caused Stanley to behave the way he did.

12

What was that sound? That...that clinking? Clanking? Ringing? Tinkling? What did you call that? Stanley frowned at the vaguely familiar sound that woke him up. Straightening up in the chair, he cracked his stiff low back. Should have, at least, accepted the bed, he thought. Chairs were not comfortable to sleep in, and the cool ground was not his area of comfort. With his desk pushed against the window, Stanley looked out into the still dark morning. He could make out a faint form of a short man with a lantern in one hand and a bucket in the other. It was the boy who accompanied Tharani. With that small memory, the whole evening of his wedding day rushed into his thoughts.

Tharani had not once turned to look at her husband throughout the entire ride to the house. Stanley had followed the cart on his horse. Surprisingly, he managed to slip into a meditative silence on the way back to his house. Not because he was feeling at peace. But more so because he was exhausted at all his thoughts. He did not want to think anymore. What had to happen has happened. What will happen, will happen. Like Swamy said, the Lord brought Tharani and him together. And so, the Lord better have a good plan for them! For Stanley knew not what he was to do with his bride!

Upon reaching the house, Tharani did not get off the cart, even after Stanley offered his hand. Only after Juggaiah placed a small footstool near the cart did Tharani disembark. She scanned the house and reluctantly followed Stanley to the main entrance. She peeked in through the doors before entering the house. Mrs.Potter offered the show her to their room, but Stanley decided to do it himself. He did not want Tharani to feel abandoned on the very first day she came home.

As was his habit of doing so, Stanley researched what his Indian bride would need when she came home. It was then he found out that, In India, there were no adjacent rooms for the master and mistress of the house, as was the norm in the elite English household. And, not wanting to offend his wife, Stanley did not make any alternate arrangements. After having spent his wedding night sleeping in a chair, Stanley regretted not making alternate arrangements. Having signaled Tharani to follow him to their bedroom, Stanley had allowed her to enter the room first. Only to have the door shut on his face. Hmm. Not what he had expected. But then, what did he expect?

Stanley stood up and stretched out his tall frame. Mrs. Potter entered the study with a tray of warm drinks. "Ah. I saw the light from under the door and thought I bring you some hot drink. Did you sleep well, master Stanley?" she asked.

The sarcasm was not lost on him, but he did not want to address it. "Thank you, Mrs.Potter. Do you know what that tinkering sound is? I thought I was dreaming, but it continued to ring. There! What is that?" he asked.

"That is Mrs.Whittamore, master Stanley" She answered, pouring some tea into a cup.

"Mrs.Whittamore?" Stanley asked, taking the cup from her hand.

"Yes. Your wife. She is a very early riser, I must say. I could not sleep a wink with her running here and there in the house." Mrs. Potter frowned. "How much of a drink did you have, master Stanley?"

A sip of the hot tea cleared Stanley's mind. "I wish I did get drunk, Mrs.Potter. I cannot seem to make any sense of my decision."

"Well, it's too late to regret now, is it not!" She said with a cheerfulness that jarred Stanley's nerves. "Must say she is a fine-looking girl. I do not believe I have ever seen such dark, beautiful eyes! Would you know what is the black paste that she lined her eyes with? I was wondering if it would make my eyes look any better? What do you think?..."

The mention of Tharani's eyes flashed two images of Tharani looking at him. One was at the temple when both of them were locked in. The second was at their wedding. Both times, Tharani's dark eyes were covered in unshed tears, and she looked like a lost child, scared and wanting help, not knowing who to ask. And on both occasions, Stanley realized he felt an instinctive desire to protect her. To hold and comfort her that everything will be alright. He stalled Mrs.Potter's questions, "What is she doing? And what is that ringing?"

"I think she is exploring the house. At least that is what it looks like." Mrs.Potter shrugged. "That is where the ringing is coming from... I was not sure what that sound was until I saw her pick up her skirt a little above her ankles to cross over the threshold." At Stanley's raised brows, she explained further, "The women here wear small bells on their feet. I observed that when I visited the village market."

"Where is she going now?" Stanley asked, moving out into the central courtyard open to the sky. He spotted Tharani running around and coming to a sudden halt on the other side of the yard when she saw him. Stanley was at a loss for words. What was he going to ask his wife?! First, he had to get her name right. "Aaa..TArani?". No sooner had he said her name that Tharani started to slowly step backward. With one forward step by Stanley, Tharani bolted out the door into the backyard.

"Well, at least we know she is scared of you." Mrs.Potter offered her opinion.

Stanley knew that was not true. During their time together in the temple, Tharani looked nervous, but she never once displayed any fear toward him. "I doubt that," Stanley said, turning around. "I will have my breakfast in the study, Mrs.Potter." After a thought, he asked, "Did she have her breakfast?"

"I am not sure. She was up and around by the time I reached the kitchen." Mrs.Potter paused in her thought. "Now that you ask, I am unsure how to ask her. Does she speak English?"

"I don't think she does," Stanley answered. He ran his hands through his hair. Lord have mercy! What was he to do?! What did he do?! Shiva better know what he has done!...cause Jesus does not know what he was to do.

Not wanting to ponder excessively on his current predicament, Stanley began to work on his future presentation of the temple complex. The temple artist had chosen coal to draw the outlines of the temple. The grey and black hues presented the enigmatic picture of the elevated dome. The black color was similar to the *kaatuka* with which Tharani lined her eyes. The sound of tinkering bells made Stanley aware of Tharani's presence. He looked up from his desk at the slow squeal of a door opening. Stanley stood up with a book in his hand and walked around to the other side of the room, making sure Tharani did not notice him walking towards the door. He did not want to scare her away.

Tharani tried straining her head sideways to see where he had walked over to. The door opened suddenly, making Tharani jump back in a scare. "Caught you!" Stanley smiled. Tharani did not find it amusing and made to run out, but Stanley caught hold of her wrist. "Don't run. I am not going to hurt you," he said, at the same time tightening his grip on her hand. "TArani...we should at least talk."

"Tharani! Tharani! Tha! Tha! Tharani! What is tArani? " Tharani spoke in Telugu, trying to wriggle her wrist free *"Leave me!"*

"What?" He asked.

"Tha!" She said.

He frowned "Tha?"

She nodded. *"Tha. Tharani."* she sniffed. She was holding back tears, and that made Stanley uncomfortable. He let go of her hand.

"Tharani?" he clarified. She nodded and ran towards the house's main entrance before suddenly stopping. Stanley followed her. Standing on the other side of the threshold was Swamy. He was dressed in formal attire with a satin turban covering his head. With hands clasped at his back, Swamy broke his firm look with a gentle smile for his daughter. Tharani ran into his arms. *"Did you come to take me home?!"* she asked. *"Please take me back home, Naana. Please!"* she pleaded. "I cannot stay here! I don't know what to do here. Please don't leave me here!" Swamy gently unwound his daughter's hands from around his neck and held her by her arms. *"This is your home, now, Ranamma. Alludu garu is a nice man. And, he will take good care of you. You are feeling this way because none of us are here for you. But, you will overcome it. You are my strong daughter, right? I know very well that you, of all*

90

people, can overcome any challenge in your way." He explained, *"Now, go and stand beside your husband.No..No. No shaking your head. Go and stand with your husband."* he commanded his daughter.
"You come in with me." Tharani invited.
"I cannot come in, till Alludu garu asks me to come in," Swamy said.
"Is this not my ho..." Tharani began.
"Don't argue, Ranamma! Go inside." Swamy chided.
Tharani clenched her fists, controlling the urge to disobey her father. She walked up to Stanley with a lowered head, looked at him questioningly, and stood a little behind him.
Stanley understood that Tharani was not happy about being here, and that was what she probably told her father. "Mr.Swamy, was it something urgent?" Stanley asked, stepping towards Swamy when he felt a tug on his shirt. He turned around to find Tharani signaling with her eyes. She turned her chin towards her father and then jerked it inwards. "*Ask him to come in,*" she said in Telugu. Stanley frowned wondering what she said "I don't under.."
"Were you going to the temple site, Stanley garu?" Swamy asked from the other side of the threshold.
"Yes. Once I had some breakfast. Would you care to join me?" Stanley asked, crossing over to Swamy. Swamy raised his hands in a namaste. "Thank you. I had my breakfast." Swamy hesitated before speaking again." Aa..if you do not mind. Your mother-in-law

has sent some sweets for you and Tharani. May I give them to her?"

"Of course." Try as he may, Stanley found it hard to be uncivil. The past days' events were tiring and rid him of any animosity he wanted to hold against this man. And, who was he to deny what a father wanted to give his daughter? No sooner had he agreed than Swamy called out to a couple of men waiting near the bullock cart. The 'some' sweets were five large bronze pots filled to the brim with sweet delicacies.

"I will take my leave now." Swamy said, "I will meet you at the temple, Stanley garu." Speaking so, Swamy said his goodbye to Tharani and left.

Entering the house, Stanley found Tharani glaring at him from under her brows. "What?" He asked with an upward tilt of his chin, not knowing why his wife was angry with him.

"You did not even ask him to come inside. Did not even offer him water. Is this how you treat elders in your country?" She muttered, knowing that Stanley would not understand what she was saying.

"Well. I do not understand you, and you obviously do not understand me. This will only work if you learn English or I learn tElugu." Stanley gestured with his hands. Tharani was not interested in what he was saying. Her stomach was rumbling, and she could not care less about what was being said to her. Let alone she did not understand what he was saying. She untied the clothes over the pots, and picking up some from each pot, she tied the sweets into the free end of her Sari, tucked it in her waist, and, swinging her long braid of hair onto her back, walked away from Stanley. "Right." Stanley sighed. "I can ask the workers for some helpful tElugu words."

13

Swamy waited patiently under the Neem tree like he had done since lunch. It was close to dinner time now. The shadow of the tree indicated the same. He knew Stanley was not very keen on talking to him. But, now that the Englishman was his Son-in-law, persuasion seemed like the only viable option for Swamy. He had sent in a field man to inform Stanley of his arrival but to no avail. Not wanting to cause a scene, Swamy spoke to some workers and waited. At long last, Stanley walked up the steps towards him, all dust and sweat.

"I am sorry to keep you waiting. We were digging out a well. I wanted to reach a certain level before calling it a day." Stanley said on approaching Swamy.

"You do not have to do the work, Stanley garu. You can tell the men what to do."

"It is faster that way." he scanned the temple area. "It would probably take another 4-5 months to clear up the whole complex, Mr.Swamy. The rains and crops have taken away most of the men. That is delaying the digging and cleaning."

"Thank you for your hard work, Stanley garu." Swamy said, "I found these papers and temple drawings. My grandfather was very interested in architecture and the arts. This is from his trunk" Swamy handed over a bundle of papers, well wrapped in satin cloth, to Stanley. "They might be of use for your paper presentation."

Stanley hesitated. To accept or not to accept. Might as well take them, he thought. He had spent months digging up these treasures in sun and rain, and he very well deserved whatever knowledge they entailed. "Thank you," he said, taking the papers from him.

"You should meet Archarya garu," Swamy spoke of their family's old priest, from when Swamy's father was the master of the house. "He was..is a priest, on our lands."

Stanley was intrigued by the suggestion. "Why should I be speaking to a priest?" he asked.

"Temples were built as a source of energy, Stanley garu. A priest upholds that energy, by performing the various rituals and prayers."

"Interesting. That will make for an interesting paper. Thank you."

Swamy smiled. Maybe, now was a good time to talk. "Stanley garu.." he started. "How is Ranamma?"

"I can only tell once I go home, Mr.Swamy." Stanley straightened his back. "It is no secret that this marriage was not the first choice for either party. It will be an uphill climb. I made a vow to respect and protect your daughter. And, I intend to keep that. Well..." he sighed, remembering what she did in the morning, "if she allows me to do so." He smiled a little tightly. "We will be fine. Thank you for the papers." He held his hand in a namaste, and Stanley began to walk away without giving Swamy a chance to speak any further.

"Stanley garu!" Swamy halted him. When Stanley turned around, "May I send Ranamma's belongings to your house. Clothes and.."

"Clothes should be fine, Mr.Swamy." Stanley nodded. As an afterthought, he added, "Could you give me a list of items that you think Tha-rani might need. I will procure them for her."

"I can send them..." Swamy started

"Thank you. I would like to buy them, for my wife." Stanley said before taking his leave.

On the small mountain overlooking Swamy's ancestral land stood the village goddess Ambika Devi temple. Having prayed to the goddess for the safety and health of her daughters, Gowri Devi waited impatiently near the steps leading into the temple pond. *"Amma!"* Tharani called out, running into her mother's arms. Gowri Devi broke into tears, embracing her daughter.

"Stop crying, silly girl! You are making me also cry." Gowri wiped her daughter's tears. *" She how your eyes are all red. Come, sit here. Did you eat anything since yesterday? "* she asked.

Tharani nodded *"I ate the sweets you sent this morning."*

Gowri frowned *"Only the sweets? Did they not give you any food?"*

Tharani shook her head *"I was in my bedroom for the whole night. Nobody woke up at sunrise. I was roaming around like a ghost in that house."* Tharani said, conveniently omitting her confrontation with Stanley.

Gowri Devi hesitated before asking her question *"And your husband? Where was he?"*

"I don't know. I locked the door as soon as I stepped into the room." She grew impatient and pleaded *" Amma, please! Take me back home. I cannot tolerate having to stay in that house with that man!"*

"What happened? Did he do anything to you?" Gowri grew concerned.

"No." Tharani said, tearing up *"I loved Bawa all my life, Amma. And now, suddenly, you tell me to accept another man, as my husband. How can I do that? I don't know anything about how they live, what they eat, what they speak. How should I even talk to him? What should I talk to him about?"*

Gowri Devi frowned at her daughter. *"Did you forget that your 'Bawa' broke the engagement? Your father had done everything he could to get the both of you married. And all he got in return was humiliation."* She held Tharani's hands *"Now listen. Whatever has happened has happened. You know and I know that your father would not do anything that he does not think is best for our family. Yes or no?"* She asked. Tharani nodded meekly. Gowri Devi tried to make her daughter see sense. *"It might be painful, but you must stop thinking about Nagabushanam. He did not own up to his love. There is no need to waste your tears and life for him."*

"But Amma..."

Gowri Devi raised her hand to stop her daughter from complaining *"Alludugaru chose to take your hand at a time when our own taunted us. You should be grateful and treat him with the respect he deserves."*

"Amma.."

"No, Tharani. I believe I raised my children well enough to be grateful to god and respect everybody. I know, and I understand, that Alludugaru comes from a different kind of life. But, a man is a man. No matter which part of the world he is from. And so is a husband. Your duty and right as a wife do not change because your husband is from a different country."

Tharani smacked her forehead. *"This is all my Karma? Why is god punishing me like this?"*

"Stop it, Tharani." Gowri Devi chided, *"Why to see it as a punishment. Maybe god is testing us. We all have to do the best that we can. Understood?"*

Tharani shook her head. *"No."* she pouted.

Gowri Devi could not help but smile at her child. *"You are my bravest girl, right? Now is not the time to show your stubbornness."* she hugged her Tharani and began gently rocking her. *"Listen to me. You are the mistress of that house. Not a person, living at your husband's mercy. Treat your husband well, and he will take good care of you. Do you understand?"*. Comforted by the warmth of her mother's hug, Tharani sniffled and became quiet, listening to Gowri Devi's voice, *"At the same time, you have enough skill to not depend on others to feed you or take care of yourself. Why did you not make any food for yourself?"*

"I was not hungry, Amma."

"Even to cry, you need energy, Tharani. Don't starve yourself for something that was not in your hands. Here.." she handed her a cloth bundle, *"I packed some food for you and Juggaiah. Tomorrow, when your husband is not home, send Juggaiah to the house. I will send some ration for you to start with. Ok?"* She straightened herself. *"Alludugaru did not want your father to give him anything. He said that he would provide for you. Whatever you need or want, ask your husband for it. Remember, you can take whatever you want from our house. But, only if it is ok with your husband."* Despite Tharani's sad expression, Gowri Devi continued, *" First, you show your husband how good you are at everything, and then, even if you get a little angry or upset, here and there, he will not take it to heart. Do you understand? Don't come to us without speaking to your husband about it first."*

Speak to her husband? How? *"But Amma..."*

Gowri Devi would not be interrupted. *"And, whatever his language is, if you learn it quickly, it will make life a little easy for you. Do you understand?"* Tharani nodded as tears rolled down her eyes. Her mother gently wiped them and said, *"Stop crying. My sweetheart, you are, right? Whenever you want to meet me, send a word to Juggaiah, and I will come to the temple to meet you. Understood? But only do it when your husband is not home. Ok?"*

Tharani hugged the bundle her mother gave her. *"How is Akka? And bawagaru?"*

"Prabhavathi is worried about you. She wanted to come with me. But, her in-laws are at home. So, I could not bring her. Her husband and in-laws will leave in a few days. They will be back in a month to take her home. I will bring her at that time. And, you both sisters can talk as much as you like. Ok?" she smiled, hoping her daughter would reciprocate. *"Now, Go home before it gets dark. And don't spend the whole night crying. Light a lamp and pray to god. Do you understand?"*

Tharani hugged her mother before walking away reluctantly. Hoping that Tharani understood what she said, Gowri Devi waved her daughter goodbye. It was hard seeing her daughter walk away in a dejected manner. As much as she wanted to hold her daughter and cry at this cruel twist of fate, Gowri had to steel herself to help her daughter see the light of the day rather than the darkness she was feeling. Gowri Devi was as apprehensive about her 'Alludugaru' as Tharani was. Her trust in Swamy's ability to do good for his family was her only hope for her daughter's better future. Wiping away the tears that she finally let loose, Gowri Devi made her way home.

14

Stanley rested his head against the water-drenched wooden beam that created a small gentle waterfall, off shooting the larger, fast-flowing one beside it. The cool water soothed his heated body. The field men working at the temple would bathe here after their work, and it was they who had shown him this beautiful alcove well hidden from the main view of the village. It worked out well for Stanley, given that it was en route to his house. One of the men handed him a few green nuts. Stanley thanked him. Soap nuts. He had never seen nor heard of this fascinating nut till he came to this place. Pinching them, as he was instructed to do, Stanley began rubbing and squeezing them between his wet palms until the nuts lathered up.

During the time Stanley had washed and changed into a fresh set of clothes, the field workers set up a bonfire near a dry area along the falls. One of the older men called Stanley, signaling him to come over to the fire. The men had roasted chicken over the fire and were enjoying gulping toddy from black earthen pots. They served Stanley some chicken in a banana leaf and handed him a pot of toddy. Taking a sound bite of the chicken, Stanley immediately reached for the cool drink to quench the fire in his mouth. The men laughed while the older man squeezed a generous dose of lime over the chicken to bring down the spice. Stanley thanked him and began to relish the food given to him. The men started to croon a song against a sun setting over the horizon. The rustic song and the toddy had Stanley become fuzzy in the head. It was when he tried to stand Stanley realized how drunk he was. "Well. So much for that," he said, looking at the men smiling cheekily back at him. "Thank you. That was very entertaining. Thank you. Thank you. And, may god help my bum tomorrow." So saying, he made his way slowly to his house.

As he approached his house, Stanley found a cloth sack lying on the floor at the front door. Two earthen lamps stood lit on either side of the closed doors. He looked around and approached the door cautiously. What was he thinking getting drunk?! Stanley chided himself. There were two ladies in the house, and it was already dark. He had always made it a point to be home before sunset, so Mrs.Potter would not be alone for dinner and after that. He walked up the few steps and stared at the sack for a minute before nudging it with his toes. Something inside moved. Stanley frowned before reaching for the sack. What in god's name was this? A shrill scream filled the air forcing Stanley out of his drunken stupor!

"Ghost !! Ghost!! The ghost has caught me!! Help!! Help!!" Juggaiah screamed, trying to scramble into standing.

"Why are you screaming, boy?!!" The sound jarred Stanley's ears. "Quite!" he yelled. The door to his house opened, and Tharani stepped out hurriedly.

"I thought it was a ghost, Akka. He looks white as a ghost, Akka! I thought it was a ghost, Akka. Akka......"

"For god's sake, stop screaming, boy!" Stanley said.

"Shh, Juggaiah. You are waking up the whole neighborhood."

"Akka..." Juggaiah was scared out of his wits. Tharani held the boy to calm him down. *"Juggaiah! Shh. It is not a ghost. It is just him. Look. See. It is just my hus..."* Tharani stopped at the point of calling this white man her husband.

"Is he alright? Are you alright?" Stanley asked Tharani and then the boy. Indicating the floor, he asked, "Why are you sleeping here?". Both Tharani and Juggaiah looked at him incredulously. The boy stood motionless. Tharani picked up the blanket from the floor and pulled Juggaiah into the house before any neighbors could see what was happening. Stanley followed and closed the door behind him. "I should get him a bed." He then sighed at that thought, "I should get myself a bed." The prospect of having to sleep in a chair at the end of a long, tiring day was not pleasant.

Tharani did not listen to Stanley. *"Go sleep in the kitchen for today. We will talk about this tomorrow,"* she told the boy.

Stanley could not help but feel a tinge of jealousy at the kind of care the boy was being shown. He shook his head to get rid of the irrational thought. Walking down the steps into the central open yard of the house, Stanley looked up at the full moon shining in. "The sky is so clear," he said and continued in a reminiscing tone. "At Whittamore house, there was a tree right outside my window. As a kid, I used to feel that the moon was playing hide and seek with me." he smiled at the memory. "Here..." he raised his hand towards the moon "..it feels like the moon is just staring at me...you know.." He looked at Tharani, standing at the other end of the central yard. She was looking at the moon and had turned to look at him when he stopped talking.

Stanley mumbled, lowering his arm down. The quietness of the house, the white moon shining, and Tharani standing in front of him was an image that suddenly filled his heart, surprisingly, with a sense of contentment. He sighed and walked toward her. "Please do not go away," he said, holding up his hand to stall Tharani's sudden move. He seated himself on the elevated edge of the yard and patted the place beside him. "Did you ea.." he paused. What was the word that the older man had taught him? Damn the drink! What was the word? Or was it a phrase? *"Thin...Thin...Thinva?"* he asked hesitantly.

Tharani did not understand. *"What?"* she asked.

"Well, so much for trying." Stanley snickered.

Tharani looked at him for a second before she walked away. "And, so much for talking." he sighed. He hung his head and rested it on the wooden pillar beside him. A few minutes later, he heard the soft jingling of bells. Tharani came back. She placed a plate of sweets and a small copper pot of water beside him. Picking up a sweet looking like a white dollar, he asked, "What is this?"

Thinking he asked what he was given to eat, Tharani answered, "*Paala Kova*"

Stanley stared at Tharani's lips when she repeated the word "Right." he said, taking a bite of the sweet "I will try saying that in the morning. This is nice." he smiled. Just what he needed, to sweeten the spice in his mouth. To his surprise, Tharani did not walk away. Instead, she looked at him as if wanting to speak. He offered her the same sweets, and she shook her head, declining them.

"Amma told me I should be grateful to you for marrying me and saving my family from disgrace," Tharani said, looking at her feet. She knew that he would not understand a word of what she spoke. And that was why she chose to talk to him. Although she understood what her mother told her back at the temple, she was not ready to accept her fate. She could not hold it within her. Since she could remember, Tharani could never keep her feelings to herself and found peace only after she had spoken

about them. "*But, why did you agree to marry me?*" she asked, looking at Stanley. "*Why did you have to agree to my father's request? If you had not agreed to marry me, my father WOULD have asked Bawa again. I would have asked Bawa again. He would have eventually agreed. I know him. I have loved him all my life, and he loves me, too.*" she cried. Stanley jerked his head back at the onslaught of words. "Ookay," He said slowly and raised his hand, indicating to Tharani to stop speaking. "As you may already know...I have no clue what you just said. But, I can say you are not happy marrying me." He shrugged his shoulders. "How else was it to happen, Tharani? Okay...Okay. You need not cry." he pleaded when Tharani began sniffing into her sari *pallu*.

Tharani would not hold back. "*You are not listening to me. And I can't understand what you are saying! How did you think this was going to work? I don't know anything about the country that you come from. I don't know anything about you. I don't even know what kind of food you eat. You cannot even say Paala kovva! What will I cook for you? And what will you eat? I don't even know your language.....*"

Stanley stood and gently reached for Tharani's hands. "Shhhhh. Calm down, Tharani," He whispered. A woman in tears made his heart flutter in a not-so-pleasant way. "Please do not cry. It cannot be that bad," he said. Tharani began to pull her hands away from his. Stanley held her chin and titled it up. "Look at me," he said. As if on cue, Tharani opened her tear-filled eyes to look at him. "I am not that bad to look at, am I?" He asked with a soft smile. Her small nose ring twinkled in the moonlight. When their eyes met, Tharani felt a pull that she could not understand. Stanley moved his eyes over her face in a de javu-like moment. The dark eyes, the sharp nose, the slightly parted lips, and a stubborn chin. Looking into her eyes, Stanley wiped her tears away. "It cannot be that bad," he whispered again.

 Though she wanted to move away, his eyes held a comfort that Tharani was seeking. That thought made her very uneasy. Stepping back from him, she walked away, embarrassed at how she felt.

Stanley let out a breath; he did not realize he was holding. Stanley had once boasted to his younger brother, Robbie, that Stanley Patrick Whittamore had never chased after a woman. Little did he know that the future Mrs.Wittamore would always run away from him.

15

"You left him sleeping on the floor?!" Gowri Devi asked, surprised at her daughter's rude behavior. Tharani pouted, miffed at her mother's response, *"I did not ask him to sleep on the floor. He fell asleep there."*

"So, you will let him sleep there?" Her mother asked. *"What should I do? I cannot carry him. And where should I carry him? It is a small house, Amma. Not like ours. It only has three rooms."* She said.

"Very bad, Tharani. What do you mean, where you should carry him? It is his house. You both will sleep in the same room....." Gowri Devi raised her hand to stop her daughter from interrupting, *"If you cannot sleep with him on the same bed, then you sleep on the floor! Whatever happens or does not happen between a husband and wife should stay within the bedroom. The whole world need not know about it. Do you understand?"*

"Who will see us, Amma? Only that older lady is at home. Who else is there?" Tharani argued.

"She and you are enough to spoil our name. Is that what you want?" Gowri Devi asked, *"That lady will go and tell you, mother-in-law, how badly you treated her son. Nobody will tell you anything. They will tell us. They will raise a finger at how your father and I raised you. About what kind of culture we have. Is that what you want your in-laws to think about us?"*

"Why would I spoil our name, Amma? This is not easy for me! I live in a small house with two people I did not know two weeks ago!" Tharani teared up. *"That house is so quiet. I am becoming mad with nobody to talk to! And you want me to share a bed with a stranger?!"* She began to cry.

Gowri Devi closed her eyes, praying to the goddess to show her a path to help Tharani. *"That stranger is your husband, Tharani,"* she said calmly and soothingly. *"See here...I understand what you are feeling and going through. But, unless you make an effort, you will not have a happy marriage. Is this how you want to live your entire life?"*

"But, Amma, I do not have any feelings for him. It scares me to be around him." Tharani pleaded.

"Don't be silly now!" Gowri Devi chided, *"You think I loved your father when I married him? Love will come with time. Satisfy a man's needs, and he will love and cherish you. You should cook what he likes or cook everything so tastily that he will lick his fingers. That man is working hard. When he returns home, you should ensure he has warm food to eat—a quiet place to rest, and a nice bed to sleep in. And you*

are very good at all of them." she tried to spark some enthusiasm in her daughter. She wiped away Tharani's tears and continued with her instructions, *"That lady, who stays with you? Your father was saying that she cooks for your husband. Why don't you learn from her? Do you understand what I am saying?"* She did not wait for Tharani's response *"And, every day, whether you like it or not, whether you speak to him or not, sit with your husband for some time. Spend some time with him...."*

"And do what?" Tharani asked sarcastically.

"Tell Hari Katha!" Gowri Devi replied, equally sarcastic. *"Stupid girl! Here, I am trying to explain to you......."*

Around this point, Gowri Devi's voice faded into the background of Tharani's thoughts. Her mother's voice became a meditative hum that brought forth emotions Tharani held at bay. Now, she allowed herself to give into the fear she had resisted—the fear of being left alone, first by her bawa and then by her parents. Tharani began to sob hard in her mother's lap. No matter what her mother said, Tharani could not imagine any future, let alone a happy one. All she had now were quiet days and lonely nights. She merely existed and hoped Stanley would tire of her lifelessness and leave her to die in peace. Gowri Devi began to caress Tharani's face. *"It will become better, Tharani. Trust my word. Your life might feel sad now, but it will improve and become better. A little willingness from your side, and I am confident that god will fill your life with happiness. Do you understand me?"*

Not wanting to talk, Tharani nodded her head. *"Now, listen to me."* Gowri Devi said, *"Your sister's in-laws are leaving tomorrow. We have some rituals for today evening.."* Gowri Devi teared up. Her younger daughter was missing out on the festivities of her marriage and that of her sister. Despite, what she was constantly telling Tharani, Gowri Devi had to suppress her urge to take Tharani back to her house. God only knew how long Tharani and her family were to bear this turmoil. *"That is why I asked you to meet me in the morning. I will send Narayanan some food for you and Juggaiah, Ok? Ask him to wait in the lane behind your house. Now go home and try to help that lady in preparing for lunch. That way, you can learn how to make their food. Did you understand?"* She asked.

Tharani nodded her head and said her goodbyes to her mother. Sitting in the bullock cart, she felt a sense of foreboding, even thinking about returning to her house. *"Juggaiah, can you take me somewhere else?"* She asked the boy.

"Where do you want to go, Akka?" he asked.

"Anywhere except home." She sighed sadly. After hearing about how she mistreated her husband, Tharani was in no mood to go back home and face the man who was the reason for her misery. She was the one who was suffering, yet her parents seemed to be least worried about her heartache. They were more

concerned about her husband's comfort. You should cook for him! He has to share your bed! Make him happy! But what about her? What about her happiness? What about her comfort? What about her heart? Not only was her heart broken, but Tharani also could not imagine her existence in the future. And here her mother was talking about learning to cook her husband's favorite dish! Why were they treating her misery so indifferently?

"There is a fair in the nearby village, Akka. Do you want to go there?" Juggaiah asked. *"I heard there is even a tholu bomma atta about Hanuman's victory in Lanka. Shall we see that?!"* He asked excitedly. Tharani smiled at the boy's enthusiasm. *"Let's go. I got some prasadam from the temple. That will be enough for lunch."*

"Akka..." Juggaiah started in a pleading tone, *"Can we buy some sugar birds?"* He asked.

"Yes. We can." Tharani said, silently reaching for the pouch tucked into her waist. She could feel a few coins resting against her skirt.

Six hours later, thunders roared overhead. Juggaiah was not the only one to look up at the dark clouds rolling up in the sky. He gently tugged at Tharani's hand. *"Akka, we should go home. It is getting dark, and it looks like it will rain.*

"We will leave once the story is over," Tharani said, not taking her eyes off the white screen of the shadow play.

"Akka, please Akka, let's go. It will be very difficult to reach home on time if it rains. Akka, let's leave. I have never ridden the cart in the rain. I will not be able to handle the bulls if the thunder scares them. Please Akka! My father will kill me if you or the bulls get sick. Let's go, Akka." He pleaded and continued to pull on her arm.

Finally, Tharani gave in to his request. *'Fine!!"* She said*, "Let's go."*

****
****
****

"Would you know where she went?" Stanley asked Mrs.Potter. He looked at the door leading to the rear end of the house. The sun hovered just above the west-facing door.

"She is always at home at this time, master Stanley." Mrs. Potter answered. She was not one to worry too much about anything. But, with Tharani, it was not the same. "This is when she lights lamps at the altar and prays."

"Did you check her room?" Stanley asked.

"Yes. I also checked near the barn. She is not there either." Mrs. Potter replied, "Blessed girl! She is making me worry! She goes to the temple every day after her lunch. The boy takes her in the bullock cart. But, She always comes back much before sunset?" she said.

"How do you know that she goes to the temple?" Stanley frowned.

"Oh. She carries that small basket of flowers and coconut. When I visited the temple, I saw most ladies bring them and make an offering." Mrs.Potter replied, feeling a little proud of her observation and deduction. "But..today, she went to the temple in the morning. She should have been back by lunch. She is usually back in a couple of hours."

"She has, probably, gone to her father's house. I wish she would let us know where she was going." Stanley ran his hand through his hair. He never really had to worry about Tharani's whereabouts until today. As long as he was home, Stanley frequently heard the soft jingle of Tharani's anklets, letting him know when and where Tharani was in the house. In the evening, the slow rhythm of the jingle moving away from his room and followed by a soft thud of a door closing shut, indicated that Tharani was retiring to her room for the night. Then, Stanley ensured all the house doors were locked before he called it a day. But, today, it was not until much later, after his lunch, that Stanley realized that the house was unusually quiet. After returning home from the temple site, Stanley immediately began preparing notes for the temple sketches. In the corner of his mind, he felt something was not right. When he started working on the drawings of the temple dome, he realized that he had not heard Tharani's anklet jingling since he came back home. He went out of his study and called out for her several times. When she did not respond, he looked for her in her bedroom. The bed was neatly made, and everything was in its place. In the kitchen, that was, as in Indian homes, outside the main house, Mrs.Potter was preparing dinner. She was unaware of Tharani and assumed that the girl was in her room. There was no sign of Tharani in the garden or around the house.

The setting sun and dark skies bothered Stanley. "I'll take the horse and go towards Swamy's house. I might catch her on the way." Stanley said. He walked out of the house and harnessed his horse. Above him, the roar of the thunder made him feel very uneasy. "God bless that girl!" he hissed under his breath. He prayed that Tharani was at her father's house.

16

Stanley jumped off the horse and pulled it into a shelter that housed other cattle. He rushed to the house and banged his fists hard on the door till it was answered.

"Stanley garu!" Swamy was very surprised at his son-in-law's presence at this time and in his soaked condition. "Is everything alright? Please come...."

"Is Tharani here?" Stanley asked, with simmering anger. He had hoped to meet her halfway to the house. But, as he got closer and closer to Swamy's home, a sense of foreboding took over him. And, with it came anger. Tharani was being very irresponsible. He had tried and was still trying all he could to make the best of their situation. He knew she needed time to adjust to the sudden and unexpected change in her life. And he was willing to give her that space and time. But she was taking it for granted. She cannot treat him like this—the fear of not knowing what happened to Tharani and where she might be added to the stress.

"Tharani?" Swamy asked, worried. "No...no..she.."

"She went to the temple in the morning and has not returned home yet," Stanley said, running a hand through his hair. "Damn that girl!" he hissed. "Do you know of any place she might have gone? Any relative? Any friend?" saying that Stanley had a sudden thought. He began backing down the steps. "Please send me a word if she comes here." He did not wait for Swamy's response and galloped away on the horse.

"Stanley garu!! I will come with..." Swamy called after his son-in-law. Swamy then called out for his wife, "Gowri?!"

Gowri Devi was serving food for Prabhavathi's in-laws when she heard Swamy call out to her, *"What? Why are you in a hurry?"* Looking at her husband's worried expression, she became tense. *"What happened?"*

"Did you meet Ranamma at the temple today?!" Swamy inquired.

"Yes. In the morning?" She answered, *"What happened? Is she alright?"* Gowri Devi began to tear up. The mention of her daughter and a worried Swamy were enough telltale signs of bad news.

"She did not go back home." Swamy replied, *"Alludugaru came here looking for her. Did she say where she was going?"*

"No...No..She did not. I told her I would send lunch with Narayana. But Narayana said that the paleru collected the food from him. I...I did not think much about...." Gowri Devi could not hold back. *"That girl*

will be the death of us! Why is she doing this? Where could she have gone? Oh lord!! Please keep her safe!"

"Ok. OK. Calm down. I will take the men and go search for her. I will go to her friend's house to check." Swamy reassured.

"Where do you think she could be? Oh Lord, please keep her safe." Gowri Devi cried. *"Please find her! Please! Let her be found; I will break her legs for putting us through this hell!!"* she declared in a mix of fear and anger.

Swamy turned to Prabhavathi, *"Take care of your mother and in-laws. I need to leave now."* While leaving the house, Prabhavathi's husband, Janardhan, joined his father-in-law in the search, even though Swamy politely declined his offer of help. Together with a couple of his servants, they left on horses in search of Tharani.

A few miles away, Stanley banged hard on the door of the only other house he had been to since his arrival in Swamy's village. He hoped that Nagabushanam would answer the door. And he did. So surprised was Nagabhushanam at Stanley's appearance at his house that he took a moment before speaking, "Stanley garu? What are you doing here?"

"Did Tharani come to meet you? Tell me the truth, man!" He questioned, without mincing words.

"What? Tharani?" Nagabhushnam quickly closed the doors behind him. Stanley's question was as

surprising as his presence. "Why would I meet
Tharani, Stanley garu?"

"You tell me! Were you not supposed to have married
her? Were you not in love with her?" Stanley spoke
harshly.

The accusations flustered Nagabhushanam. He
straightened his spine in defense. "Stanley garu, I am
a respectable man. Please....."

"Tharani has not come back home."

"What do you mean?"

"She went to the temple in the morning and did not
return home. Please! If she has come to meet you,
please tell me. I need to know that she is safe. Did she
meet with you?" The worry in Stanley's voice was
very obvious.

"No, Stanley garu," Nagabhushanam replied. "I have
not met or seen Tharani since your wedding." He
sincerely wished he could have offered more.

"Would you know where she could be?" Stanley
asked, almost knowing what the answer was.

"No. I.."

Stanley did not wait any longer. He said a quick thank
you and left. Riding towards the temple on the
mountain,

he met Swamy on his way back. "We looked around
the temple, Stanley garu. There is no sign of
Ranamma. My men are searching the path to the
temple. She likely left the temple safe." he tried to
assure Stanley.

"I cannot think of any other place she would be at," Stanley said.

Swamy tried to rein in a concern that had bothered him since Stanley came to his place. "Stanley garu, please go back home. Your caretaker is alone at home. Please go back. I will look at a few other places and inform you if I find anything."

"She did not go to Nagabhushanam," Stanley said, even though Swamy did not voice his doubt.

An uncomfortable silence descended between the men. Relieved as he was, with that bit of news, Tharani was still missing. Swamy was upset at his daughter's disappearance but not as much as he was embarrassed at what his son-in-law was going through. More so, because Swamy felt that it was upon his request that Stanley agreed to marry Tharani. "Please, Stanley garu." Swamy requested, "Go home.... " he was interrupted by a man running towards them with a flame torch in his hand. Picchaiah, Stanley's stable man, was running towards them, calling out to Stanley.

"Stunle *babu!* Stunle *babu!"* Pichaiah called out, panting. He then began to talk with matching gestures to make sure Stanley understood what he was saying." Potter *amma asking you. She worried. Come home. Come . Come."* he said, pointing towards the direction of Stanley's house.

"*What happened, Pichaiah?*" Swamy asked, *"What happened to Potter amma?"*

Pichaiah looked a little perplexed at the question. A caretaker of cattle on Swamy's lands, Picchaiah's whole life revolved around cattle and horses. Only things that affected them concerned him. Hence, he was oblivious that Tharani was not home all day long. But he was very aware that the bulls were missing from the shelter. And that Mrs.Potter was upset. So upset was she that she had rushed him without giving him time to put out the water for the bulls or to make them warm. *"Nothing happened to her, sir. She is alright. She just wanted Stunle Babu to come home immediately."*

*"*Why?" Stanley asked after being filled in by Swamy about Pichaiah's request. Swamy voiced the same. Pichaiah replied to Swamy, "*I don't know, sir; as soon as Tharani amma went to the house. Potter amma came running to me as if the house was on fire!"*

Stanley caught Tharani's name. "Tharani came back?!"

"Yes," Swamy said. Both the men rode quickly towards the house, leaving behind an even more confused Pichaiah.

Meanwhile, Mrs. Potter was staring into the night sky, praying that master Stanley would return home. Stanley, generally, did not lose his cool in any situation. But, she also knew the heat of the temper that Stanley could let off if prodded into that state. A glimpse of it was witnessed when Stanley mounted his horse with his lips held in grim lines. Now, with

Tharani's situation, She knew it would be an explosion. Mrs. Potter wrinkled her gown into her fist, waiting anxiously for Stanley's return.

Stanley, Swamy, and Janardhan rode up to the house. Only Stanley got off his horse. Mrs. Potter rushed down the steps. "She came back about a half hour after you left, master Stanley." She whispered loudly, "She is fine. Nothing to worry about." She smiled nervously, praying that Stanley would not react aggressively. "Shall I set out dinner for all of you?, Riding in the rain can be tiring." she tried to play down the emotion and smiled at Swamy and Janardhan. "Mrs.Wittamore is alright. She is." she smiled at Swamy.

"Thank you," Swamy said. "We will leave, Stanley garu. Rannamma's mother will be quite worried. I need to calm her down with the news. I am sorry for the trouble Tharani has caused." he apologized.

"You don't have to be sorry, Swamy. Thank you for the search party. Thank you." Stanley said, with a slight nod towards Janardhan. Both the men rode away. Stanley turned to Mrs.Potter, his face in grim lines. "Where is she?" he asked, entering the house. "

"In the kitchen." she hurried behind Stanley, who was already halfway through the house. "Master Stanley, you should change into dry clothes. You are dripping wet. Master Stanley! listen to me!" She caught his arm and halted him. "I do not believe she realizes what she has done!" Mrs.Potter tried to reason with

Stanley. "She is a naive girl. She might not have thought..."

"Well, she should have thought, Mrs.Potter!" Stanley said, "Naivety is not an excuse for such behavior!"

The loud talk brought Tharani out of the kitchen. After reaching home, Tharani hurried to prepare some warm food for Juggaiah as he got soaked in the rain, riding the bullock cart. She did not want him to catch a cold.

The thunderous rain and darkness scared Tharani, reminding her of the day she was trapped at the temple with Stanley. She chided herself for being selfish. She should have learned her lesson, but no. She had to behave like a complete idiot. What is the point of blaming karma for her fate? When she was stubbornly putting herself and others in danger. Her mother was right. She was an idiot! There was not a moment, till she reached home, that Tharani did not scold herself. All the way home, Juggaiah was brave and managed the bulls and cart with a talent way beyond his years. Tharani had promised him and herself that never again would she insist on staying out beyond sunset. And, wanting to make it up to him, Tharani instructed Juggaiah to dry himself up and come to the kitchen for dinner. She hurriedly prepared rice, *Pappu,* and *Payasam,* for the boy. She was serving him the food when the loud voices outside the kitchen made her want to find out what the fuss was. Standing there was Stanley, pale as a ghost, wet clothes clinging to him. He must have got wet in the rain, coming back home, she thought. What was he thinking about not changing his clothes and arguing with the lady? She should fetch him a towel to tell him to dry himself up. Tharani, with her head lowered, moved around them towards her room.

"Where were you?" Stanley asked, trying very hard not to raise his voice.

Unaware that the question was directed at her, Tharani walked past Stanley.

"Don't walk away from me, Tharani!" Stanley caught her arm in a vice-like grip. "Where do you think you are going?" he asked through gritted teeth.

Tharani winced in pain. "*What? Leave me!*" She tried prying his fingers away.

"Where in the hell did you go?! Stanley yelled, "We were looking all over the village for you! And, here you are, without a bother about what you have done. You selfish chit!! "

"*Why are you yelling at me?! Have you gone mad?! *" Tharani yelled. What was wrong with this man? Why was he behaving like this?!

"You are driving me mad, Tharani!"Stanley shot back, "Do you not have any sense?" He said, jamming a finger at her temple. "Can you not tell us where you are going? Or, be back home before it gets dark?!"

Tharani got offended at the implied action of her being mad. "*Yes! I am mad! Mad to think of getting you a towel to dry your hair..*" she pointed at his head "*so that you will not catch a cold. Mad to think that I*

*will bring you some warm milk! Mad to follow
Amma's words! I am mad!"* she said.

"What?! What are you saying?! Stanley frowned,
frustrated at not being able to follow any of what
Tharani said.

"*I don't know what you are screaming at me
for?"* Tharani was equally frustrated.

So frustrated was Stanley that he was not thinking
straight. He pulled Tharani into his study, put an ink-
dipped quill in her hand, and pointed at a paper on the
desk. Tharani looked at the quill in her hand, the
desk, and Stanley. They glared at each other for a
minute before Tharani gave up and began writing on
the paper. She thrust the parchment at him and
walked out in a huff. Stanley clenched his jaw and
looked at her and then at what she had written. His
jaw slackened, and his frown cleared. He let out a
breath of defeat. What was he thinking?

'*What do you want me to write*' Tharani had written,
very neatly, in Telugu.

"Right." Stanley sighed. He pulled out a bottle of
liquor, stashed in his desk.

17

"The whole world is only worried about him. Do you know how scared I was?" Tharani pouted at Mrs. Potter. *"I was only going to get him a towel. For that, he screamed at me as if I killed somebody!"* Mrs.Potter looked down at Tharani. The girl was seated just inside the kitchen door and had been in the same place since Mrs.Potter began preparing breakfast. Tharani had not spoken anything till she offered her some freshly baked bread. The girl had taken a bite, and that was when the waterworks started. Mrs.Potter was a little alarmed at the beginning, but not knowing what and how to respond to what was being said, she silently continued to prepare breakfast and looked sympathetically at Tharani whenever the girl turned towards her in the heat of the speech. The bread was baked, the eggs prepared, and the milk ready. But the Tharani was still pouring her heart out. Mrs.Potter arranged the breakfast on the tray and picked it up to go. Tharani stood up and blocked the doorway. "Now, my dear, I understand you are upset. But this is not the way to

behave. I need to get Master Stanley his breakfast."
Tharani reached for the tray. "Oh. Mrs.Wittamore,
you do not have to do this." Mrs.Potter let go of the
tray when Tharani tugged at it. "Well! she sighed.
"As you wish. I am going to come with you, though.
Lest he thinks it is my idea." She waited for Tharani
to step out of the door and followed her to Stanley's
study.

Tharani did not wait to knock on the door. Instead,
she stepped over the threshold and tapped her foot on
the floor. Stanley turned around at the sound of the
jingle and raised his brow at seeing Tharani. But it
was Mrs.Potter that he addressed. "I am not interested
in speaking to her, Mrs. Potter," he stated, looking
back at the papers on his table.

"Well, you can try telling her that, yourself, Master
Stanley." Mrs. Potter said. She walked into the room
and approached him. "Me thinks Mrs. Whittamore is
very sorry for what happened. The poor girl has been
crying her eyes out all morning and complaining.
Though, I do not know what she has spoken," she
finished.

"Me thinks," Stanley spoke sarcastically, "Sorry is the
last thing she is feeling right now."

"Master Stanley! How can you say so? Yes, she did
give us quite a scare yesterday... But, you are being
unforgiving yourself!" Mrs. Potter said.

"She is boring holes into my back, Mrs.Potter."
Stanley signaled towards Tharani, "I can feel the heat
of her stare, and you tell me she is sorry?"

And, rightly so, Tharani was glaring at his back from under her brows. She held the tray firmly in her hands and had not moved after stepping into the room. Why was he behaving like that? Not only had he yelled at her, he had not even looked at her properly since the morning. Much as she liked ignoring him, Tharani was not used to being ignored. Not by her family or by him. Up until yesterday, Stanley had always smiled at her. Now, god only knew what crime she had committed. The whole house was uncomfortably silent, and nobody was doing anything. Little did she realize that her guilt made her feel desolate.

Not knowing where to put down the breakfast tray, Tharani walked up to the table and cleared her throat. Stanley glanced at her and continued with his work. Mrs. Potter sighed and walked out of the room. Miffed at not getting any response from Stanley, Tharani shoved the tray into his hands and began clearing the table of all the papers. "What do you think you are doing? What is the meaning of this?" Stanley got irritated.

"*How long should I hold the food and stand? Now hold it till I clear the table.*" Tharani said.

"Tharani?! Lord have mercy!" Stanley stood up with the tray in his hand.

Ignoring his irritation, Tharani took the tray from his hand and placed it on the table. She indicated him to eat. Turning around to walk out of the room, Tharani saw, through the window, her father walking towards the house. She ran towards the door. Stanley, too, saw

Swamy and took a bite from his toast before walking out to meet his father-in-law. At the entrance, Tharani stood still. Swamy did not enter the house, nor did he greet his daughter. Instead, Swamy looked blankly into the house. Stanley frowned. Swamy ignored Tharani and stood silent till he saw Stanley.

"I hope I am not disturbing you, Stanley garu. I just wanted to make sure everything was alright." Swamy said.

Stanley came up beside Tharani. "Good morning, Mr.Swamy. Please come in. Join me for breakfast." he said.

Swamy folded his hands in a *namaste*, "I will come in.." he said, stepping inside. " But I will not be able to join you for breakfast. I have already eaten."

Swamy paused as if hesitating to continue. "Juggaiah told me they went to the next village, to a fair. It started raining on the way back. And got late coming home."

"Oh. Well, that was not a safe course of action." Stanley looked at Tharani. She was looking at her feet and fidgeting with the door. Did she know that Swamy was narrating her outing yesterday? "Why don't we sit down and talk about it?" Stanley offered.

Swamy continued to ignore his daughter. "I will not keep you longer, Stanley garu. " He took a step closer to Stanley and bowed his head in embarrassment. "Please accept my apologies. You have been very patient and kind with my daughter. There is no excuse for what she did yesterday. I can only blame myself for her rude behavior."

Seeing her father bow his head in front of Stanley, Tharani felt immense guilt. She had always felt proud of her parents and wanted them to feel the same about her. It was one of the things that drove her to excel in whatever was asked of her. Well, that was until she was asked to marry this man. A broken heart made her blind to the anguish of her parents and their effort to rectify an unpreceded situation. The sight of her father bowing down in embarrassment filled her heart with sadness and her eyes with tears. She could not bare to face her father and ran into her room."

Swamy did not even look at his daughter. But Stanley was left standing in an awkward standoff. He understood Swamy's feelings but seeing a girl in tears upset him more. "Please do not apologize, Mr.Swamy. Sometimes, we cannot predict how people feel, catching us off guard. This situation must be quite stressful for her, too, and as such, I cannot blame her for wanting to take a small break." He smiled hesitantly. "Why don't you have some toast with me?" he offered again.

"I will have to decline. I will go now. Prabhavathi's husband and family are leaving today for their village. It is not a good time to take her along. Your brother(by marriage) will come back after a month to take his bride home." Swamy said, "Will you be going to the temple today?" Swamy asked.

"Ah.No. The men have instructions to clear up the mudslide from yesterday's rain and to build flood banks around the smaller Ganesh temple we cleared last week. After what happened yesterday, I thought it would be better to spend some time at home. To make sure that everything is ok." Stanley said.

"Of course," Swamy said before taking his leave. Stanley returned to his study and finished his breakfast. He got immersed in his temple presentation and worked on it for an hour or so before he realized that he had not heard Tharani's anklet's jingle. He went to her room and saw her lying prone across her bed, with her head turned to one side. He sighed in relief and slowly closed her room doors, leaving only a crack of space open. Closer to noon, Mrs.Potter inquired if he wanted the lunch served. "Can you bring it to the study, Mrs.Potter?" He asked.

Mrs.Potter left to bring him his lunch. A few minutes later, He heard, Tharani's anklet jingle stop at his doorway. Stanley did not look up. The chime continued into the room "Right." Stanley sighed. "What do you want, Tharani?" he asked, turning around. Tharani stood silently behind his chair, holding his lunch tray, her head bowed. Stanley stood up, not wanting to risk a spill on his papers. "Uhh...Wait...." he said.

Tharani quietly placed the tray on a chair and waited for him to clear the table. She then moved the tray from the chair to the table, walked to the door, and stood there in silence. Stanley did not know what to make of this quiet behavior. Was it the silence before the storm? Or had the storm been silenced? "Did you have your lunch?" he asked cautiously, making a gesture of taking food to his mouth.

Tharani looked at him with sad eyes. She cried herself to sleep and felt emotionally exhausted to indulge in any conversation. Realizing that her father was ashamed of her filled her with sadness, and with it came tears.

"You do not have to answer the question, Tharani," Stanley said, not wanting to start a flood of tears. "You want to stand there while I eat? I am sure it will not bother me. Just...Just.." He smiled. "Aaa...I will have my lunch," he said.

"Please forgive me for how I behaved yesterday. I did not do it on purpose. It will not happen again." Tharani tried to hold back her tears. *"I...I ..will not let my father be ash....."* The tears rolled down.

"Lord, have mercy!" Stanley walked up to Tharani. The more he wanted to ignore her, the more he had to address her. "Please stop crying, Tharani." After the rain-soaked search yesterday, followed by the shout-off, Stanley wanted to stay home and make sure Tharani was not too upset to run away from home again. What he did not expect was, Tharani deciding to sit in his study and be upset. What she was crying about, he was not sure. However, his well-founded guess was that she was thoroughly upset at being ignored by her father. "Come. Sit here." he guided

Tharani to a chair. He knew that any conversation now would be a moot point as neither would understand the other. So he opted for the only universal solution to sorrow. He pulled out the bottle from his desk, poured some of it into a glass, and offered it to Tharani.

Tharani looked at the burgundy liquid, smelled it, and took a sip cautiously. The taste tingled on the tongue. She then gulped the remainder down. "Slow, girl!" Stanley warned.

An hour later, Mrs.Potter and Stanley stood at the end of the bed in Tharani's room.

"What were you thinking, Master Stanley?!" Mrs.Potter admonished. Tharani's soft snore stopped her from saying further.

"Obviously, I was not, Mrs. Potter." Stanley smiled childishly, looking at his wife sleep. "You think she will be alright?" he asked.

18

"Potter amma!!" Pichaiah exclaimed, *"You should be gentle. The cow will kick you!"* he said, very upset that Mrs.Potter was trying to experiment with his cows. Why could she not stick to cooking food instead of torturing the cow by milking it?

"Lord! Pichai! You are going to scare the animal!" Mrs.Potter said, not understanding what the sudden outburst was all about.

Tharani laughed. She understood Pichaiah's concern. She reached for Mrs. Potter's hand and stopped her from tugging at the cow. Pichaiah's tolerance ran low with anybody who mishandled animals, and he was getting more agitated with each passing moment. Mrs.Potter had walked into the cowshed, fascinated at seeing Tharani milk the cows. She, too, wanted to try it, and Tharani let her try. The demonstrations, as was evident, were not well understood. Tharani held Mrs. Potter's fingers and squeezed them gently, showing how much pressure should be applied and in which direction. She then kept her hands on Mrs.Potter while the older lady was able to, for the first time, squirt some milk into a pot placed under the cow's udder. "Lord, be merciful!" Mrs.Potter exclaimed delightedly. "Is that not wonderful?!" she said with pride. Tharani smiled at her like a teacher proud of her pupil's work. Pichaiah, on the other hand, could not care less.

"Only a few more minutes, Laxmi. You have a lot of patience, right?" Pichaiah soothed his cow. *"This white woman has a cow's body but not the gentleness. You don't have to worry about her from tomorrow. Ok?"* He gently rubbed his hand over Laxmi's neck. Stanley stood at the door, opening into the backyard. He could hear the laughter of Mrs.Potter and Tharani. They looked like they were having a good time, bringing a smile to his face. Tharani had not gone out of the house, even once, since the night of the incident. She spent her time in the kitchen, helping Mrs.Potter with the English meals. While the main course was made to Stanley's liking, Tharani made an Indian sweet for dessert. She had continued to bring him his tray of food until a week ago when Stanley decided that all of them would have their meals together. Whether they genuinely enjoyed each other's company or did not have anybody else, Tharani and Mrs.Potter bonded well over the weeks. So much so that when Stanley returned home every day, he found them playing a chalk-drawn hunt-and-chase game on the steps of their house. There was peace in the house. And that did not sit well with him. Tharani's obedience, though calm, felt forced and

unnatural. She smiled at him but did not communicate anything. There was a certain restlessness about her that Stanley sensed. After dinner, Stanley retired to his study every day to journal his day's work. Tharani would bring him a pitcher of water and sit on one of the chairs. She would not speak to him unless he spoke to her first. She did not disturb him. She would merely sift through the books and look at them as if trying to read. Although both were not sure they understood each other's words, they learned a few words from both languages.

Stanley placed the letters in his pocket and walked towards Tharani. "If my ladies are done with their morning chores, shall we go?" he asked Mrs.Potter. "Oh. Of course, Master Stanley." Mrs.Potter said. Stanley helped Mrs.Potter stand up. "But, first, would you care to have a glass of *paaa..*" She looked at Tharani "*loo?"* she completed. Tharani smiled. Pichaiah smacked his forehead, unseen by the others. "I suppose that means milk?" Stanley asked. Mrs.Potter nodded excitedly, "Yes! Yes!" "Maybe later, Mrs.Potter. If we leave now, you need not suffer the afternoon sun." Stanley said. "Oh.We are ready, sir."

Stanley smiled at Tharani, who shyly lowered her head. Stanley took Mrs. Potter's arms and led her out, "you did not tell her, did you, Mrs.Potter?" he asked. "Oh no, master Stanley! I would not be able to tell her even if I tried." Mrs.Potter smiled.

Tharani did not realize she was to join them until
Mrs.Potter, sitting in the bullock cart, patted the place
next to her. Stanley stood behind Tharani and
indicated to her to get into the cart. Tharani shook her
head and made to go back into the house. Stanley
blocked her way. "We are going to the temple site,
Tharani." he informed, "*Goo-
dee.* We.Are.Going.To.The.*Goodee,*" he said slowly.
Tharani shook her head again and said the easiest
English word, "No!"
"Alright," Stanley said. He lifted Tharani off her feet
and, very effortlessly, seated her in the bullock cart
beside Mrs.Potter. "Given our limited vocabulary in
each other's language..."He placed a finger on
Tharani's lips to stop her from protesting "...It is quite
pointless to argue, my dear." he said. As their eyes
met, Stanley was unsure if he wanted to say anything
further or had forgotten what he wanted to say.
Small as that gesture was, it was the first time Tharani
experienced an intimate touch. It sent a certain shiver
down her neck. Yet, it did not occur to her to move
his hand away. It was not until Mrs.Potter cleared her
throat that Stanley realized he had just shared a
moment with Tharani. "Right," he said, clearing his
throat. "We shall leave." he walked around to his
horse, leaving behind a blushing Tharani.
As the cart made its way through the village's main
street, Stanley looked for Varaha Swamy. Tharani's
younger brother was waiting under the banyan tree.
Seeing Stanley and the bullock cart moving along the

road, Varaha Swamy waved enthusiastically. The movement caught Stanley's eye, and he waved back at Varaha Swamy. In reply, Varaha Swamy smiled and disappeared into the street behind the tree.

When they reached the temple site, Stanley helped Tharani and Mrs.Potter off the bullock cart and showed them around the temple area. In the past weeks, Stanley and his men had uncovered wide steps leading into a structure deep into the earth, which he learned was a man-made pond. While Mrs.Potter marveled at the elaborate temple complex, Tharani was more interested in the intricate figures carved on the pillars. A while later, the three walked over to a makeshift seating area under a tree. Swamy was waiting for them, along with Varaha Swamy.

"Ah.Junior Swamy! Thank you for the message." Stanley said, shaking Varaha's hand, "I hope your sister will not be angry with me for doing this."

Swamy frowned. "Did she not behave well with you, Stanley garu?" he asked, wondering what his daughter had done now.

"Oh, no. No." Stanley corrected, "Quite the opposite, I must say." He looked at Tharani. Seeing her father continue to ignore her, Tharani assumed her father was still angry at her. She slowly slid behind Stanley and stood calmly. Such obedience from Tharani bothered both Stanley and Swamy. "She has been very quiet over the past two weeks. How long will it last?" he asked Swamy.

Swamy knew his daughter very well. The obedience was her way of saying she was sorry for what she had done. It was never a complete surrender. "As long as you let her, Stanley garu." Swamy tilted his head a little to glance at his daughter and smiled. It was still hard for Swamy to come back home and not have Tharani greet him at the door. Prabhavathi had always been a shy and responsible child who idolized her mother. Varaha was the son who would take over all the responsibilities after him. Although Swamy loved all his children, Tharani was the child who lived life with cheeriness and abandonment; Swamy loved to see and enjoy. Though she did everything asked of her, Tharani did not feel the need to be perfect about everything like Prabhavathi did and did not fuss about making mistakes. Tharani told Swamy what she would not share with her mother or sister. An adventurous child, Tharani never worried about getting into trouble because Swamy was always there for her.

"You are not allowed to get angry at me!" she had once yelled at him as a four-year-old when Swamy tried to discipline her. And that, Swamy thought, was what he now regretted. Tharani needs to know that she cannot keep behaving so irresponsibly. When his daughter stared back at him from under her brows, Swamy cleared his throat and straightened himself. Tharani would never learn if Swamy kept defending her actions. "Thank you for bringing her, Stanley garu," he said. "Her mother will not let me live in

peace if she does not see for herself that Ranamma is alright. I told her that our child was in your good hands. But a mother's heart cannot be satisfied with words."

"Of course, Mr.Swamy. She was roaming the house like a lost soul. The outing will help lift her mood. Where is Mrs.Swamy?" Before Stanley finished his question, Tharani saw Prabhavathi getting off a bullock cart that had arrived at the site and ran towards her.

"*Akka!*" tears rolled down Tharani's cheeks as she ran into her sister's arms. *"Now? Now you found time to come see me?"* she cried.

"Shh. Stop crying." Prabhavathi wiped her sister's tears. *"I wanted to come to meet you the day after my in-laws left. You only did not come to the temple. How many times did amma send word for you? You never came."*

"Why should I come?" Tharani asked, *"You know; Nanna did not even talk to me the next day when he came to our house? And, amma. She would have just scolded me!"* she pouted like a small child.

A hand reached out from between the drapes of the bullock cart and whacked Tharani on the head. "*I would have broken your legs for what you did! Stupid girl!*" Gowri Devi chided without getting off the cart. She tried to peek out and could not see where her husband was standing. "*Where is your father? And alludu garu? Are they still standing there?*" she asked Prabhavathi, who nodded her head in answer. "*Ok.*

Ok. Both of you get in. I told your father I would take you to the market."
Tharani was too excited to be with her family to take her mother's banter to heart, which she never did. She did not get into the bullock cart, though. "*Wait. Potter amma came with us. She and I will come in the other cart. I will go to bring her."* Tharani ran back excitedly. She caught Mrs.Potter's hand and signaled her to follow.
"Mrs.Wittamore! Where are we going?" Mrs.Potter asked.
"Do not worry, Mrs.Potter. My wife wants to take the girls to the market." Swamy said, then turned to Stanley, "With your permission, Stanley garu."
"Of course. of course."Stanley said, "Though I do not think my permission is needed, Mr.Swamy." He looked at Tharani, tugging Mrs.Potter along. "Will you be alright, Mrs.Potter?" he called out.
"I will be fine, Sir," Mrs.Potter replied, trying to keep the hat on her head.
On reaching the cart, Tharani realized she did not have her money pouch. She looked back, called out to her father, and sprinted toward him. When she came up to him, without a word or even looking at her father, Tharani reached into her father's pockets and pulled out money, as she had always done. But, for the first time, Swamy gripped her hand and stopped her. "*Ranamma,"* he said in a firm tone, "*You are not a child anymore. Is this how you will behave in front of your husband?"* he chided. All the sorrows she had

forgotten flooded back to Tharani, and so did tears.
Stanley did not understand why Swamy had scolded
Tharani. But, looking at the coins in her hand, he
realized that Tharani probably wanted money to
spend at the market. But why was Swamy angry?
Tharani lowered her head and sniffed to stop the tears
from rolling down. Why was her father treating her
like this? Will he ever be good to her again? She
dropped the money back into his pocket and pulled
back her hand. Without a glance at either of the men,
she turned around and began to walk away. Stanley
saw a small water container on his desk and picked it
up.

"Tharani," he called out and walked up to her.

"Here.." he said, handing over the water pouch when
Tharani looked at him. "You will need this. It is a hot
day." he said, "And..." he reached into his pockets.
"Take these too. I am not sure if that is sufficient. But
that is all I have now." he took her hand and placed a
few coins in her palm. Tharani shook her head, but
Stanley closed his fingers over her hand and walked
her to the cart. He helped her into it. "And, come back
home," he said with a wink.

19

"Is there something you would like to confess, Mrs.Potter?" Stanley asked, waving the letter at her. The older lady blushed in embarrassment. She recognized the writing on the letter, but that did not mean she had to confess. In her defense, how was she to know that things would not be as bad as they seemed at that time? She acted out of concern for Mr.Stanley and was not sorry. Although seeing master Stanley hold the letter, Mrs.Potter wished she had not been in a hurry to write one herself. Plus, it was not uncommon for people her age to be forgetful. Yes, and that is what happened. She forgot to tell master Stanley about the letter she had written. "I do not understand what you mean, sir," she said.
Stanley raised his brows at Mrs.Potter's reply, "This is a letter from my mother, Mrs.Potter."
"Oh. How lovely." Mrs.Potter tried to sound nonchalant. "Why are you surprised about that, sir? It is quite natural for a mother to..."

"My mother does not write to me, Mrs.Potter."
Stanley said, "Especially not a letter that has
URGENT written on it." he waved the letter again.
Mrs.Potter dabbed some sweat off her brow. "You are
being dramatic, master Stanley."
"Robbie congratulated me on my wedding." He said
flatly.
"As should he, sir. After all, you did marry."
Mrs.Potter tried to remain calm.
"I never wrote to him about the wedding, Mrs.Potter."
Stanley's voice turned interrogative. "I did not write
to anybody."
"Well...it is.."
"Mrs.Potter," Stanley said slowly.
"Oh, Master Stanley! What was I to do?!" She cried. "
We have nobody here. I felt you were being tricked
into marrying that girl. I could not stop you..."
"Mrs.Potter." Stanley stalled Mrs. Potter's rambling,
"How, may I ask, was my mother expected to stop the
wedding?"
"I do not know, sir!" she cried. "I was feeling
desperate and helpless. The only thing I could think
of doing was to write to the Dowager countess."
Stanley sighed. "Well, so much for that."
"I am truly sorry, master Stanley." Mrs.Potter begged.
"I hope everything is alright back home."
"Not exactly." Stanley answered, "The number of
letters I have received does not bode good news."
"What do you mean, sir?" Mrs.Potter felt a little
alarmed at the sound of bad news.

"Well, I have letters from Mother, Robbie, and the girls," Stanley replied. His uncle and aunt were killed in a tragic accident, leaving behind four children, two young daughters, and toddler twin boys. As the older brother, Stanley's father had become the children's guardian, and after his father's death, Stanley was now the sole guardian of his young cousins. Due to his expeditions, Stanley had left his younger brother, Robert, in charge of his estate affairs, with the twins being a given addition to the responsibility. Having read through the letters, it became apparent that it was time he returned to resume his duties as the Earl of Whittemore, which meant that Tharani would be going back with him.

Stanley had deliberately withheld the news of his marriage from his family, knowing full well the theatrics that his mother would display. He wanted to break the news to his mother and be there personally to handle the consequences. God alone knew what Robbie was going through! Stanley's younger brother was not a very patient man when it came to handling anybody's heightened emotions. The twins were enough to drive any man over a ship into shark-infested waters. Robert was a man of few words, and so was his letter.

'Dear brother,
You better be in good health. I am expecting you back before the London season starts. That is as long as I will tolerate this mad house you have left in my charge. Mother has been uncontrollable since

the letter from Mrs.Potter. She has decided to station herself at Whittamore house till your return. The girls, sweet and angelic as they are, need to be taken off my hands. I do not fancy getting myself shot in any duel I will have to challenge in their honor. Besides, you always had a better aim than me. And the boys! They are irreparable. Congratulations on your wedding! I hope the girl is worth the fight. Get back soon, Your ever-faithful brother, Robbie.'

The girls were of an age to be introduced into society. As the guardian, Stanley would do the honors in the coming London Season. He had planned his travel accordingly. What he did not expect, though, was to get married himself. Well, what had to happen, happened. Now, what needs to be done, needs to be done. Stanley sighed. "Well!" he said. "Today will be a long evening, Mrs.Potter. I will try to be home earlier. Where are you and Tharani going today?" he asked.

"Oh. Nowhere, sir. We did not make any plans for today." Mrs.Potter said. "My old body does need a break." Tharani had picked up a bunch of *Kondapalli* toys when she went to the market with her mother and sister. The toys were wood figurines of people and scenes depicting village people and their lives, like a farmer in a field, a husband and wife, a well, a river, a potter, a temple, and so forth.

After dinner that day, Tharani and Mrs.Potter sat him down and made him guess what each wood carving depicted. Having been shown real-life versions of the toys, Mrs.Potter could confirm the accuracy of Stanley's answers.

In the following days, Stanley understood why Tharani and Mrs.Potter were excited about the toys. Every day since then, he found one toy on his desk. It was Tharani's way of letting Stanley know where she was taking Mrs.Potter that day. "When did you become old, Mrs.Potter?" Stanley smiled.

"Oh! master Stanley!"Mrs. Potter blushed. "Well, I better get back to the bread before it becomes a biscuit." she walked away with a smile.

Stanley walked towards his study. After going through the temple sketches, Stanley had written down questions he wanted to ask the temple architect. When he entered his study, Tharani, standing at his desk, turned around in a scare. Stanley paused in his step. What he saw in front of him was a vision. It was the first time he saw Tharani with her hair untied. Long, black hair, reaching beyond her waist, was curling around her shoulders and face. The free end of her pink sari draped around a dark green skirt lay loose over her left arm. Standing in front of the window, the sunlight shone through the thin fabric and outlined the silhouette of her slender waist. Stanley's gaze went from her face, where pearl rings dangled from her ears, and then to her neck. A pearl and ruby necklace rested over a slightly heaving chest.

Further down, a gold waistband emphasized the curve of her hips. Stanley's gaze rested there for a moment until Tharani moved closer to him. She was holding a small wood-carved temple in her hand that she held out to him.

"Ahh..that..that ..is your wai...no.No!It.aah. Is," Stanley frowned. What happened to him?! what is the name of that?! "Goo...Goo. Temple. *Goodee!"* He got it right, finally. "You are going to the *Goodee,*" he stated. Tharani nodded. "Oh good.good." Stanley was not feeling quite as good as his words. He had never faced difficulties communicating with the fairer sex or enjoying their company. But trying to do the same with Tharani was proving an uphill climb. The difficulty was not in accepting the attraction he felt for his wife. He did not want to overwhelm the girl, though. He wanted to woo...

"Today is my birthday. Amma wants me to come to the temple. I will come back before lunch," Tharani said. While Stanley's gaze made her stomach tingle and her toes curl, it was very frankly appreciative. And that made it difficult for Tharani to stand in front of him. She could not also stop a blush from warming her cheeks. Having informed him of where she was going, Tharani placed the temple toy on Stanley's desk and quickly walked past him.

The jingling anklets broke Stanley's thoughts. He closed his eyes. "She is my wife! She is my wife!" he affirmed in a loud whisper.

"She sure is." Mrs.Potter said with a smile as she walked into the room with a tray of warm drink for Stanley.

Stanley did not open his eyes. "Sometimes, Mrs.Potter, it's rather uncomfortable to realize that you are the only person I can talk to over here," he said. All he heard in response was soft laughter fading out through the door.

Later that afternoon, Tharani stood outside the temple while Pichaiah loaded a set of stacked containers her mother had brought along into the bullock cart. *"I made your favorite chicken curry, Pullihora, and bobattlu. The last three boxes are for alludu garu. I made the chicken curry with less spice. When you give it to him, add some nayyi and give. That way, he will not find it that spicy. Did you understand? I also made him some laddu and payasam...*

"It is my birthday. And you made him two sweets and one for me? Why like that?" Tharani asked, frowning at her mother. Why should he get more attention than her?

"Because he needs the energy to bear with you." Gowri Devi smiled at a pouting Tharani. *"Now stop your silly questions. You are a married woman. You should take good care of your husband, and he will take good care of you. Understood?....."*

"Enough, amma, From the time you married me off, that is all I hear. Keep your husband happy. Do this for him! Do that for him! Have you ever told him to make me happy?" Tharani asked.

"Don't make me scold you on your birthday." Gowri Devi said. *" We had a nice pooja in your name. You got the gift from your father...."*

"But naana did not come," Tharani said sadly. How long was her father going to be angry with her? Gowri Devi adjusted and tucked a loose curl behind her daughter's ear. *"Your father has always been very proud of his children. But, When you went away like that and alludu garu came to our house looking for you, your father felt very embarrassed by how you behaved. It will take him some time to overcome that. Tharani, you have to remember. People will question your upbringing with your behavior. Do you understand?"* She asked. Tharani nodded in answer. *"You should go back home,"* Gowri said to her daughter.

Tharani said her goodbyes to her mother and climbed into the bullock cart. The site at which Stanley was working fell between the hilltop temple and her home. When crossing that path, Tharani had a thought, *"Pichaiah, turn towards the temple*?" She said.

"Again, amma?"

"Not the Devi temple. Shiva temple. Where HE is."

"Oh. HE? Ok. Ok." Pichaiah smiled and turned the cart towards the temple site. When they reached the

spot, Tharani hopped off and began unloading the carrier. Pichaiah came around to help her.

"*Here.*" She pointed at another carrier in the cart. *"That one is for Potter amma, you, and Juggaiah. You take that home. Have your lunch, and then come back."*

"Ok, amma. Shall I go and call Stunle babu?"

"No, no. You go. It is getting late for lunch. I will call him." She said. Pichaiah left after placing the carrier on a blanket under a tree, out of view from the site. Tharani searched for Stanley and found him near the Garba gudi, talking to the temple architect. She walked over and stood a little away from him.

"*Listen.*" She called out.

Stanley and the architect, an old family friend of Swamy, turned around at Tharani's voice. "Tharani?" Stanley smiled. "Well, this is a nice surprise."

Tharani smiled back and then, turning towards the architect, folded her hands in a namaste, *"Namaste Achary garu. How are you?"*

"I am good Tharani amma. How are you?"

"I am good. Today is my birthday. I went to the temple and came. Amma sent some sweets and food for us. So, I thought I would bring him lunch."

"Oh. Nice nice. May God bless you with a long and healthy life, and by next Ugadi, may you have a healthy baby boy!"

Tharani blushed at the blessing. *"Please have lunch with us."* She offered.

"No, no, amma. My wife too must have sent..."

Stanley coughed. Pleasant as the conversation was, Tharani was here for him. But she had not even looked at him properly yet. He waved a hand in front of his face. "There is a lot of dust in the air," he said, coughing again. He moved to stand beside Tharani and faced the architect. "Alright, sir. We should probably call it a day. It is.."

"Yes. Yes. You should have your food." Achary garu said.

Stanley looked at Tharani. "You brought me lunch?" he asked. Tharani nodded and pointed towards the tree. "Ah. We are having a picnic. How nice. I am hungry!" The architect smiled at the couple and left.

"Alright, Ranamma! Shall we go?" He asked. Tharani noted the way he called her. Nobody, except her father, called her by that name. Should she tell him that? It sounds like her father said it, so it should not matter, right?

As she mulled that thought, she led him to the tree where the carrier awaited them. "All that food for the two of us?" Stanley asked as Tharani opened the boxes to display the food. "And it is all rice! How do I eat that, Tharani?" He asked, pointing at the food and indicating the mixing of rice with the curry. Tharani thought for a second. She then washed her hands and began mixing rice with curry and a generous dose of *nayyi*. Stanley sat on the blanket and watched his wife make small rice balls. After it was done, Tharani gave the plate to Stanley. "Now, this is convenient!" He said, picking up a rice ball.

They shared the meal and enjoyed the sweets. A full
and satisfied Stanley lay down on the blanket while
Tharani began packing away the boxes. Tharani's foot
peeked out from under her skirt. Stanley curled his
finger under the anklet, looking at the intricate design.
Tharani froze in her position and held her breath.
"This is beautiful." He said. He ran his finger along
the curve of the anklet and slowly slipped it over her
ankle. "I am not sure how lo..." Tharani tried to jerk
her foot under her skirt, but Stanley gripped her foot.
"No..please.." Stanley hung his head and sighed. It
was not the right time or place. He let go of her foot
and rolled onto his back. "Oh, lord! Have mercy!" He
whispered loudly. "What are you doing to me,
Ranamma?!" He asked, placing his hat on his face.
Tharani was finally able to breathe. *"What did I
do?"* She asked, hearing her name.

20

"Elbow! Elbow Stunle babu!" Pichaiah yelled from outside the mud circle. "Footu! Footu babu!" he yelled again.

Stanley elbowed Basawayya in his chest. That loosened the burly man's grip around Stanley's neck. He wrapped his foot around Basawayya's ankle and tripped the man. Stanley waited for his opponent to roll onto his back before he jumped atop Basawayya and held him down with the point of a wooden dagger. "*Shachav Po!*" he said with a victorious grin.

Meanwhile, Pichaiah rushed over to the judge's table to argue about the unfair and unethical neck grip that Basawayya had used. Stanley walked over, too, and spoke in a breathless voice. "What happened, Pichaiah? Did I not win?" he asked.

"You winoo, Stunle babu!" Pichaiah said happily and then frowned, looking at Basawayya. "He. Badu! Necku *holding* badu!"

Stanley shook his head. Only recently did he realize that Pichaiah had started speaking to him in English.

One just had to disregard the U at the end of the words. He turned to find Swamy approaching them. "How do I ask him not to argue every time?" Stanley asked Swamy.

"You do not ask, Stanley garu." Swamy said, "You tell him." Swamy dusted some of the mud off his hands and chest. "*Pichaiah, stop fighting and get me another shirt,*" Swamy ordered. Pichaiah immediately nodded his head and went away to fetch what was asked.

Stanley smiled at Pichaiah. This animal lover had introduced him to this Wrestling club of sorts. Initially, Stanley was just an audience member, while Pichaiah and, surprisingly, his father-in-law wrestled in the mud arena. It took some time for Stanley to adjust to this new persona of Swamy. The jaw-clenching, grunting, thigh-slapping people punching Swamy was a stark contrast to the mild-mannered, *panche-clad* village elder Stanley had known thus far.

Swamy and Stanley spoke of the wrestling technique in England, and It was then that Swamy realized that Stanley could wrestle. Thus began the weekly matches.

"So, when are you leaving Stanley garu? Swamy asked.

"In the morning. After breakfast. It will be a week's ride to Hyderabad. I am also to meet up with the artist for the sketches of the tunnels. Then my work is done." Stanley explained. He had finally received

word from the Nizam's secretary about the sketches.
The letter was more polite this time. But, it raked up
some old wounds and the conflict. Stanley decided
not to burden his brain and go with how he felt at the
moment. Right now, he felt good after the match. He
also knew that going back home, Pichaiah would
massage the soreness out of his body, which he was
looking forward to.

"Oh. I will tell Varaha to come tomorrow. He will
stay till you come back. " Swamy said. Knowing that
Stanley would be out of town for a month, Swamy
had asked if Varaha could stay at his place for the
duration just so that the ladies had company.

"Thank you." Stanley said, "I did not want to leave
the ladies alone without each not knowing what one
was saying to the other." He smiled and said goodbye.
When Stanley and Pichaiah reached home, the later
ran into the backyard to make sure Juggaiah had
heated water for Stanley's bath. Stanley walked into
the house to fetch his clothes.

"Ah! Master Stanley. Did you have a good bout, sir?"
Mrs.Potter asked.

"It was good, Mrs.Potter," Stanley replied and looked
around the house. Tharani was usually the one to
greet him when he came back home. She always
brought him a small pitcher of water. Given the heat
in this country, Stanley now understood why people
always offered water first. Today, though, she was
not to be seen. "Where is Tharani?" he asked.

"Oh." Mrs.Potter looked towards the end of the house, leading to the master's bedroom. "I presume Mrs.Wittamore is in her...in your room, sir. The bed has just arrived. The men placed it in the room."

"Ah! The bed!" Stanley smiled and walked towards the room. He had ordered a bigger bed from the local carpenters. If Tharani wanted to maintain distance, so be it. He was done sleeping in the study. On reaching the room, Stanley found Tharani looking at the bed, standing at the foot of it. "That looks well made and sturdy," he said. Tharani turned around in fright. What would she do if he...He slowly began unbuttoning his shirt and leaned into the door frame. "What do you say, Ranamma?" he said in a husky whisper. "Should we..." Tharani rushed over and slammed the door shut. "Right!" Stanley sighed and tapped on the door. "Open the door, Tharani?" he called out.

"No," came the reply.

"I am not sleeping in the study anymore, Tharani," he warned. All he heard was the jingling of anklets. Any further action was prevented by Pichaiah, calling out to Stanley for the massage. Before leaving, Stanley tapped on the door and said, *"Nee, Naa Mancham!* Only *Nee* No."* Inside the room, Tharani understood what Stanley implied. She wiped the sweat off her forehead and throat. What she was unable to comprehend was the sudden rush of emotion she felt when Stanley was close to her or when he looked at her the way he just did. It has been happening more often in the past few days. She had mixed feelings about wanting to stay away from him and, at the same time, be with him. She held her head, unable to make sense of her feelings. God! she prayed. How was she to deal with this? She cannot throw her husband out of the bedroom. She could not bear her father or mother being called names because of her behavior. *Bagwanthuda!* What was she going to do?

Her answer came in the form of her brother. Varaha Swamy had brought along the finest horse from Swamy's stable, which had the endurance for long-distance traveling. Along with a list of homes that offered travelers to stay for the night on the route to Hyderabad. Tharan insisted that Varaha stay for dinner, and following that, she asked him to stay for the night.

"It is very late," she said, holding her brother. *"Stay back for the night. You can go home in the morning."* she insisted.

Varaha looked outside the window at the setting sun. *"It is not very late, Akka. I can go..."*

"Keep quiet, Varaha!" Tharani admonished, *"It will be dark when you go home. What will amma say? That I could not let my brother stay at my home for one night? That I sent you off into the darkness?"*

"But Akka.." Varaha protested.

"No, but. Pichaiah can inform amma that you are here for the night."

Varaha frowned at the silliness of what Tharani was suggesting. Before he could say the same to his sister, Tharani turned to Stanley. "Varaha stay?" she asked. Stanley, leaning against one of the pillars in the central courtyard, watched the drama his wife was putting on. She had avoided looking at him or being near him for most of the evening. She did not bring him the sweet after dinner, as she usually did. She sent Varaha instead. And now, she also intended to avoid her husband for the rest of the night? Stanley smiled slowly. "Of course, he can!" he said. Tharani could not contain her happiness. She excitedly held Varaha's hand and, saying her thank you to Stanley, turned towards their room. Stanley stalled her "Tharani, can you bring me some water?" he asked. Tharani nodded and went to the kitchen. "Junior Swamy!" Stanley clapped the young boy's back. "Let me show you to your bed," he said and promptly directed Varaha to the study. "Here. I am afraid this is all I can offer now," he said, showing the hammock-style bed in his study.

Not sure what he was supposed to make of the situation, Varaha spoke apologetically, "I am sorry, Bavagaru. I can go back home. It is not very late."

"Don't be silly, Varaha. If it is not a bother for you to sleep here, I am happy for you to stay. I am sorry that I cannot offer you a better bed." Stanley said.

At the same time, Tharani walked in with a pitcher of water. Noting her brother sitting in the hammock, the smile on her face dimmed. She looked at Stanley. "He sleep here?" she asked. Stanley nodded in confirmation and walked out of the room. Tharani put down the pitcher nervously and wrung her *pallu.* Over in their room, Stanley stretched himself on the new bed and sighed. "Ahh! How I missed you," he said, relishing the feel of the flat mattress under him. Tharani walked in hesitantly. Stanley sat up in bed and smiled.

Tharani placed the lantern on a table. "You sleep here?" She asked nervously.

"We sleep here, Tharani." Stanley corrected.

"No." Tharani shook her head. She cannot ask him to leave the room and have her brother witness it. "You here. *Me there."* She pointed outside the door.

"No. You and me here." He insisted.

"No." She persisted.

Stanley narrowed his eyes at Tharani. Hmm. How about a change of adverb? "Yes." He said, patting the bed beside him. Tharani almost ran out of the room. Stanley reached the doors before her and shut them with a thud. "No, Tharani." He shook his head in disapproval. " You cannot keep running from me." He said with a stern expression. He could not hold to it for long, though, and broke into a smile. "I have a reputation, my dear. And, I intend to keep it that way." He stepped slowly towards her. Tharani backed away from him, not sure of his next move. "You cannot still be afraid of me?" He asked politely, not taking his eyes off her. "What have I done to make you feel that way?"

Tharani could feel her heart beating against her chest. She curled her toes to mute an excitement she was feeling scared to express. Trying to dissipate the tension in the room, "Ok. *I here* sleep." She said.
"Good," Stanley replied.
The continued gaze of her husband made Tharani restless. She turned away from him and reached for the bedpost to steady herself. Her heartbeat raced for a moment, and she froze when she felt Stanley place his hand on her. Her heightened senses could smell and feel him stand close behind her.
Stanley lowered his head and smelled the Jasmine flowers in Tharani's hair. God! This was messing him up! He gently pushed her hair to one side and, slipping his hand around her waist, kissed her neck. Tharani held his arm around her waist and tightened her grip as Stanley continued to kiss her neck. Stanley slowly pulled down the sleeve of her blouse and kissed her shoulder, caressing her arm with his other hand. Tharani began to shiver.
"Shhh," Stanley whispered into her neck. "Let go, Tharani."
"I...I..." Tharani could not handle the heightened emotions anymore. She was becoming breathless. She tried to pull away from Stanley, but he did not let go.
"Why?" He asked, turning her around to face him. He held her in his arms. Many questions arose in his mind. Questions he had. Questions he wanted to ask. But he waited. He would not force himself on

Tharani, but he was not letting go. Not yet. Not till she said something.

Tharani closed her eyes and lowered her head onto Stanley's chest. She stayed that way till she found herself easing into his embrace. After a long, paused moment, she raised her head to look at Stanley. He looked down at her and smiled. "See. It is not that bad." He said, gently tugging a stray strand of hair, behind her ear.

Tharani did not understand what Stanley said. Nervous as she was, Stanley's arms around her made her feel warm on the inside. She liked the warm feeling but wanted to move away from him simultaneously. This man was causing a storm of emotions within her! But then, how could she also feel safe in his embrace? He was driving her into confusion! "I sleep, please?" She asked.

Stanley let her go and stepped back. "Of course." He said hesitantly. He watched as Tharani picked up a blanket and began spreading it on the floor. "Oh no, you are not." He said, grabbing the blanket off the floor.

That ticked Tharani off. She was trying to accept and be his wife as much as she could allow herself to. Why was he putting hurdles in her way? How was she to suddenly start sleeping with him? How can he not understand that? *"What are you doing?"* She asked and tried tugging the blanket away from him.

Stanley did not let go. "My wife will not be sleeping on the floor!" He stated. "You sleep here." He pointed to one side of the bed. "I sleep there." He said, pointing to the other side of the bed. "I no touch you." When Tharani began to shake her head, he raised his hand to stop her. "Shake your head at me, Mrs.Wittamore, and I will just have to kiss and suck the fear out of you." He warned. "There is a limit to how much patience I have!" Tharani looked at him incredulously. Stanley sighed. Why did he bother? He tugged the blanket and pulled her closer. "You sleep on the floor, and I kiss you." He said, pointing at the floor. "You on the bed, I no touch." He gestured. "Kiss?" Tharani asked, hearing a new word.

Stanley held her face and, before Tharani could react, kissed her on the cheek. "Kiss." He said. Tharani held her cheek and slowly sat on the bed. She did not want to utter another word, fearing another explanation. "That is much better," Stanley said and walked to the other side. He lay down and closed his eyes. What had he expected? She needs time, is what he told himself. 'You are losing your touch' is what Robbie would have told him. Damn!

"Mudhu."

Stanley opened his eyes. "Did you say something?" He asked Tharani. She was lying with her back to him. "What?" He asked when she did not answer. Tharani turned to face him but did not look at him. She pulled the pillow in front of her.

"Kiss. *Mudhu in Telugu,"* she said without looking at him.

"Oh." Stanley smiled.

The following day, Stanley stood in the central courtyard of his house, hands held behind him, and said goodbye to Mrs.Potter and Varaha while waiting for Tharani to emerge from the kitchen. She was gone when he woke up, and he barely saw her till breakfast. "Take good care of my ladies, junior Swamy." He said to his young brother-in-law.

"I will take good care of them, Bavagaru," Varaha promised.

Stanley finally saw Tharani walk in from the backyard. He waited for Tharani to come up, but the silly girl stood behind her brother. "Right then," Stanley said. At the same time, he saw Pichaiah move swiftly across the backyard. " Aah, Mrs. Potter, I think the cow's got your petticoat again?" Stanley said, looking into the backyard. "Quick, Swamy! Help Pichaiah."

"Oh no, no, no, no! Wretched cow!!" Yelled Mrs.Potter hurrying out into the backyard right behind Varaha.

Seeing them run, Stanley grabbed Tharani by the arm and muted Tharani's scream with his lips. The sudden excitement of the kiss replaced the shock of being held. Much as she wanted to protest it, Tharani gave in. It felt right. And good. Stanley swayed Tharani into a corner and deepened the kiss. When he heard the voices returning, he let go leaving a shaken Tharani gasping for breath. "There! Your *mudhu!"* He whispered in her ear. He placed the flower he was holding, in her hair and leaned in again. "When I come back, more *mudhu,"* Stanley promised with a wink.

21

"I cannot do it, amma." Tharani moaned in a weak voice. *"I tried everything. Everything."*
"Shh." Gowri Devi said soothingly. *"You don't need to think about that now. Just have some water and rest. You are tired."* Gowri Devi said, wiping away the tears and the hair covering Tharani's face.
"I am very scared, amma!" Tharani cried into her mother's shoulder. *"I did everything you told me. But, she is not improving. She did not eat anything in two days! I don't know what to do! I don't know! I cannot do it anymore! I am scared she will die! Even He is not here! What should I do?!!".*
Pichaiah brought Gowri Devi a wet towel. *"Tharani amma has not slept properly in two weeks, ammagaru,"* he said, almost apologetically. *"Day and night, she is taking care of that lady and even Juggaiah. She cleans the house if she is not feeding or bathing them. No matter how much I tell her, Tharani amma is not resting as she should. Do you think she is getting the fever?"* he asked.

Gowri Devi placed the cool, wet towel on Tharani's forehead. Tharani moaned softly and closed her eyes again. *"The older one and Tharani both had it when they were kids. She will not get it again. She is just tired with all the work that she has been doing."*Gowri Devi said, *"When did Jugaiah's father come?"*

"He came yesterday evening and took the boy away, amma. I thought that, at least with the boy being taken care of, Tharani amma would get some rest. But Potter amma's fever would not come down. Tharani amma was with her the whole night, trying to bring down the fever. I told her I would stay awake, but she would not let me stay."

"Hmm." Gowri Devi gently tapped Tharani's shoulder, lulling her into sleep. *"She needs to rest. Do you know when Alludu garu is coming?"* she asked.

"Tharani amma said that he would be coming today, amma. Shall I go to the village border and wait for him?" he asked.

"No, No!" Gowri Devi said, *"Now is not the time to go to the village border. It has hit us hard this time, Pichaiah."* she said, *"I have not seen it like this since their childhood. My worry is about Alludu garu traveling. Almost all of the villages east of the river have been affected. And that is the way that way home for him. We don't even know if he has had it before or if their land has this problem or not."* she said, looking at Tharani. *"Is the lady in her room?"*

"Yes, amma," Pichaiah said.

"Bring the food and the medicine from the cart." She instructed. Walking out of the room, she looked at all the doorways lined with branches of neem leaves. The periphery of the central courtyard looked decorated with greenery. *"When did you change the neem leaves?"* She asked.

"Yesterday, amma."

"Good. After you bring the food, boil water for a bath. Add the neem leaves and turmeric. Alludu garu should bathe before coming into the house. It is good that the bedrooms are on different ends of the house. How are you feeling?" Gowri Devi asked. Most of the adults born in their village were not affected by *Ammoru*. Growing up, they had it at one point or another during their childhood, as did Prabhavathi and Tharani. The kids and people not native to this region were severely affected. Gowri Devi had heard of the outbreak a couple of weeks ago. Having dealt with it earlier, she was not very alarmed about the situation. When she heard that the English lady was down with a fever, Gowri Devi immediately rushed to her daughter's house. Varaha had never had it. His staying at his sister's place and the fact that Tharani would not know what to do, made Gowri Devi disregard the tradition of not visiting a daughter's house when the son-in-law was not home. It did not help that Swamy was not at home. A day earlier, Swamy had accompanied Prabhavathi on her first journey away from home to her husband's house. And now, since the outbreak, there was no knowing when

Swamy would return. Gowri Devi was as worried as her husband, knowing that Swamy had the *Ammoru* previously and was generally of a healthy constituency.

By the time Gowri Devi made it to Tharani's house, Juggaiah was already shaking with fever, and Mrs.Potter had an outburst of spots all over her body. Gowri Devi had seen both of them and instructed Tharani on how and what to do for them. Tharani was also given instructions on cleansing the house and isolating the two affected people. The following day, Varaha developed the symptoms and has been sick since. Gowri Devi could not come back but regularly checked on her daughter when bringing the medicines to the lane at the back of the house.

"I am fine, ammagaru. It is Tharanamma that I am worried about. She has been working like an ox. It would have been better if Stunle babu was here."

"He would not know what to do, Pichaiah." Gowri Devi said as a matter of factuality. *"She will have to learn to handle difficult situations. Now, go. Get the food."*

Gowri Devi cleaned up in the kitchen and checked on Tharani. With Tharani still sleeping, she carried a small bowl of soupy rice into Mrs.Potter's room and sat beside her. *"Potter amma."* She called out gently. Mrs.Potter moaned in response. *"You need to have some food. Open your eyes and see."* The older lady moaned again. *"No sleeping. How will you get better if you do not eat?* Mrs.Potter moaned. *"Alright then, open your mouth,"* Devi instructed. Not seeing or hearing a response, she pinched Mrs. Potter's nose shut. Once Mrs.Potter opened her mouth to breathe, Gowri Devi shoved a spoonful of rice into her mouth. *"There. Eat."* And thus, Mrs.Potter was fed. Gowri Devi walked into the backyard and found Pichaiah feeding the cattle.

"Feed yourself before feeding them." Gowri Devi said.

Pichaiah smiled. *"Seeing them eat fills my stomach, amma."*

"That you will say. But it will not give you strength. Understood?". Pichaiah blushed at being reprimanded by his mistress. *"Tharani and Potter amma are sleeping. They are fine for now. When Alludu garu comes, make sure he bathes and eats. Then, come home. I will pack dinner and keep. Understood?"* She then turned towards the house and recited a small prayer for the village goddess and then left for home.

A couple of hours later, Stanley smiled at the sight of his house as he rode up the street leading home. The thought of a good bath and the vision of his doe-eyed wife brought a sense of relief to his aching body. His journey back home was tiring, to say the least. In contrast, the trip to Hyderabad was as pleasant as the distance and weather would allow.

After the sketches were given to him, Stanley was invited to a dinner with the Nizam. The dinner, in its ambiance and abundance, though it reminded him of the king's ball, was on a different level with the kind of generosity shown to the guests.

The Nizam lived the life and how? Stanley has seen a diamond-studded ring slip off Nizam's finger. Stanley did not expect the Nizam to bow down to pick it up, but what surprised him was that the Nizam refused to wear any jewelry that dared to fall off him. He, quite causally, told the servant, who picked up the ring, to keep it for himself.

The other surprise of the evening was when the Nizam's minister approached Stanley, along with a man with a brooding look. Stanley had never seen the second, older gentleman, who looked like a landlord but did not belong to the Nizam's court. As the minister introduced him, he did not have to think any further.

"Stanley *sahib*, this man is related to you." The minister said with a cheeky smile.

Stanley raised a brow and smiled. "You will have to excuse me if I did not recognize you from my wedding, sir." He said, holding his hands in a namaste.

"He is your sister-in-law's father-in-law." The minister said.

The brooding man smiled and whispered something to the minister. "He wants to confess a matter." The minister told.

"Confess? To me?" Stanley frowned. "Whatever for?"

"Stanley *Sahib*, the men outside your house on the day of the wedding, were his men." the minister explained. "He wanted to make sure you did not run away from the wedding." The minister laughed hard enough to mortify Stanley. The brooding man, though, looked a little apologetic.

"I am not a man to usually force myself on people, Stanley garu. But, I hope you understand that it was not only the matter of Tharani's life but also my family's pride that was at stake."

Given the brass wine holder he was holding, neither the minister nor Chalapathi Rao could make out the force Stanley was exerting on it. As was the norm with him, Stanley began having a mental dialogue. First, a relief that Swamy had nothing to do with it. Anger that this stranger of a man thought he could coerce him into marriage. Stanley sneered at the thought. There were several things that he wanted to say. *How dare you? Who do you think you are? What made you think I could not fight off your men? Did you actually believe that YOU could force me into a marriage? In my country, I would have challenged you to a duel. You would not have survived to speak off!* "Well, unhappy as I was with that arrangement, please be assured that a few burly men would have hardly forced me into a marriage that I was not agreeable to," Stanley said.

Chalapathi Rao bowed slightly after the minister interpreted Stanley's words. *"When you denied all the gifts Swamy garu had planned for you, I realized that you must have known my men were at your house. Since then, I have not had an opportunity to confess*

my interference, either with you or Swamy garu.
When I came to know that you would be here, I
traveled to tell you so. Given that you are my son's
age and the circumstances of the wedding, I hope you
see it as a fatherly concern to make sure things
happened for the best."

Stanley understood every word but had not yet
learned to be as fluent in Telugu as he would have
liked. "Well..." what could he say now. "Fortunately,
things have taken a good turn. And I am a happy man,
sir. I will not credit you with my good fortune.
Having said so, and since you are part of my in-laws'
family, I believe we should assume you did not do
what you have done. Especially since the outcome
would not have been any different, irrespective of
your interference."

Chalapathi Rao laughed after the translation was
done. Tapping Stanley on the shoulder, the older man
said, *"We do not apologize to our sons, Stanley garu.*
I am happy to see that Swamy made a wise decision.
You are a good man." having said that, Chalapathi
Rao and the minister moved to a different group of
people.

Stanley was mildly miffed for the rest of the evening,
but the next day, as time passed, he began to feel
more light-hearted about his situation and began his
journey back home in a good mood.

It was when he crossed the river that he could feel the
gloom in the air. He saw people burning bodies in the
graveyards in the first few villages he passed. Unlike

in his country, the cemetery was always at the edge of the village and was more of a cremation site than a burial ground. It became a familiar sight with every passing village, which worried Stanley. Something was wrong. People did not smile like they usually did. They were maintaining distance. Stanley did not bother to take a rest at the usual *sathram.* Instead, he galloped as hard as the horse could handle and did not slow down till he reached his town, while the sun was still high in the sky.

The familiar sight of the open doors to his house was a relief. He trotted his horse into the shed for the cattle and disembarked. "Ah, Pichaiah! Nice to see you, man! Rub down the horse and give it some water, will you? He was a very good boy!" he instructed, gently rubbing the horse's neck.

Pichaiah was not his usual smiling self "You good Stunle babu?" he asked.

"Well, I am tired," Stanley said. He felt the same gloom that he experienced while riding through the villages. "Is everything alright, Pichaiah? You don't look too well," he asked.

"Me *parvaledu,* Stunle babu. Our *Ammoru.* Very angry. People falling."

Stanley frowned. "What? I do not quite understand what you mean."

"Leave it, babu. You bath first. I boil water. Come. I *madhena* you." he gestured.

Stanley laughed. "Oh, I am looking forward to that! Let me say hello to my ladies first. Then I will be right out." he said and walked towards the house. Tharani had just woken up and walked into the central courtyard at the same time Stanley walked in. Seeing him, Tharani did not care about the present circumstances.*"You came back!!"* she cried out in joy and ran straight into his arms. Her long, untied hair bounced behind her.

Stanley wrapped his arms around her and whirled her before resting his back against a pillar. "Ahh! Happiness to a tired soul!!!" he smiled tenderly, leaning in and kissing her hard and long. Tharani was not precisely the blushing girl he had last seen when he pulled back. Instead, she was frowning. "What happened, darling?" he asked, pushing some loose hair strands off her face.

"You hot," Tharani said, teary-eyed.

"What?!"

22

God! It was a lot of effort not to shake the whole bed
with the shivers. Tharani draped Stanley with another
blanket and began rubbing his cold feet. "You do not
have to do that' moaned Stanley.
"Shh. Sleep." was all Tharani said. Her struggle to be
calm and not cave in was visible.
Her happiness at seeing Stanley lasted as long as their
kiss. Stanley's body was warm, and his eyes were
slightly dazed. Despite her protests, he denied having
a fever. It was the heat of the day; not his body, is
what he said. His body was all dusty from the long
journey in the heat. He could feel the grains of dust in
his mouth. He was tired, and his body ached from the
trip. Even Pichaiah could not convince him against a
bath. Stanley never fell sick. He had his occasional
cold, as such. But, was never down with fever. Hence,
his firm belief was that he did not get the *Ammoru*.
After the refreshing bath and a warm meal, Stanley
wanted to rest awhile. An hour later, he woke up to
chattering teeth and a rocking bed. Tharani's fear,

earlier calmed by her mother, returned in its ugliest forms. Mrs.Potter's condition was heartbreaking enough. The thought of Stanley going down the same path was a fear she could not handle. Despite Pichaiah's reassurances, Tharani broke down in the kitchen. Pichaiah's relentless talking and hard-hitting words of buckling up at the time of crisis calmed Tharani's anxiety. She finally saw that she needed to act instead of getting paralyzed with fear.

"Tharani...." Stanley tried again.

"Shh. Sleep. Please." Tharani did not look at him. Pichaiah walked into the room with a small water tumbler in his hand.

"Oh, no, no, Tharani! I am not drinking that again."

"Shh!" Tharani said. "Drink. You good in two days." Stanley scrunched his nose, "I have been drinking that for four days now!"

"Drink Stunle babu! Your body hot. Drink this, and you become cold." Pichaiah pleaded.

"Cold and dead is what I will be," Stanley said with a sniff and snarl. He regretted saying that as soon as he did. Tharani looked at him in shock and turned pale.

"No..No..Tharani. I am sorry...." Tharani ran out of the room before Stanley could pull aside the sheets.

"Darn it!" he cursed. "I did not mean it that way, Pichaiah," Stanley explained at the latter's disapproving look. "I did not...It is just an expression..." He sighed, "I will go fetch her."

"Tharanamma, alright, babu. She feeling *bayyam*. Potteramma not good. You drink *Kashayam*. All bad run from bady." He said, holding up the potion to Stanley.

"Leave it on the table, Pichaiah. I will have it. First, let me go and find....." He tried to heave himself off the bed. Damn the affliction!! Stanley could not remember the last time he felt this weak.

"Stunle babu. No get up. I bring Tharanamma." Pichaiah offered.

"*Nobody needs to fetch me.*" came a curt reply from the doorway. *"Pichaiah, go and feed your animals. I will give him the Kashayam."* She said, walking up to the bed and taking the tumbler from him. Walking out, Pichaiah closed the doors behind him. "Please drink." She asked Stanley.

"Do I have to?" Stanley asked. Tharani nodded.

"Alright, then." Stanley gave in. He did not want to cause any more anguish to Tharani. From the day he returned, Tharani and Pichaiah were always at work. Be it taking care of them or cleaning the house. He had never seen any girl of Tharani's birth work as hard as she did.

His body shivered with the taste of the concoction. He shuddered at the last sip of it and laid back when done. Only God knew how Mrs.Potter had been drinking this for the last couple of weeks. "How is she doing?" He asked Tharani.

The thought of Mrs.Potter's condition brought tears to Tharani's eyes. She shook her head, looking away from Stanley, "No good." She said.

"Do not worry, Ranamma." he smiled, holding her hand in his. In his present condition, and having seen her, Stanley was not feeling as confident as he usually would. But, Tharani need not know that "She has robust health. She will recover before you know it. Who else would have endured the kind of journey that I put her through in this country? Now, why don't you rest here with me?" When Tharani began protesting, he tugged at her arm. "No. You need the rest as much as we do. Come here. Lay down." Feeling quite tired, Tharani did not protest as much. She lay down beside Stanley, facing him. All the while, Stanley held her hand.

"Right." He smiled, "what was I saying?" He asked, closing his eyes and slipping into a slumber. Tharani smiled and slightly curled the tip of his mustache. She, too, fell asleep to the rhythm of his soft snore. Later that evening, Tharani stood beside a sleeping Stanley, tightly clutching a small, black leather-bound book. She knew Stanley needed the rest. But she was crumbling inside. Her legs felt weak, and so did her heart. Tears would not stop. Unable to hold back any longer, she shook Stanley awake. "Listen!" She said in a trembling voice.

"What?! What happened?!" Stanley woke up. Tharani held the book to his face, trying to wipe her tears at the same time. "What is that? What happened, darling? Are you all alright? He tried to sit up.

"No." Cried Tharani. She pushed the book into Stanley's hand and stepped back, agitated and restless

"Pray." She said, holding her palms together. "Please. Pray." She pleaded.

Then, Stanley realized that Tharani had handed him Mrs.Potter's bible. In disbelief, he got off the bed and hurried towards Mrs.Potter's room. Tharani followed. "No.No, no. Mrs. Potter?!" He whispered aloud, sitting down beside her. Mrs.Potter's body was pale, in sharp contrast to the redness of the rash. She was as still as a dead body if not for the feeble whimpering.

"Mrs.Potter?" Stanley called out gently. The older lady did not answer. "Nanny!" He tried again. "I dare you to leave me, nanny." He said. It was a phrase he had often used as a child whenever he got into trouble, even after Mrs.Potter had warned him of it. Mrs.Potter whimpered again. Stanley reached for her hand. Mrs.Potter turned her head ever so slightly.

"You will be alright, nanny. Be strong. We are not going to let you go. There is so much more to see." Standing behind him, Tharani broke down again, "I try. I try all." She said with tears rolling down. She held on to Stanley's shoulder. "Pray." She said again, "Please."

Stanley merely nodded and opened the bible to read. He was not a man of prayer himself, but he never questioned people's belief in its strength. While Stanley read from the bible, Tharani held his hand and bowed her head in prayer.

After two days of 'will she or will she not' agony, Mrs.Potter finally started showing signs of recovering. Feeling better himself, after a good night's sleep, Stanley went to check on Mrs.Potter.

Mrs.Potter was not in her bed, though. She was standing near a lounge chair, gently leaning over Tharani's sleeping body, covering her with a sheet against the morning chill.

"Ah. I see you feel good enough to start your chores, nanny." He whispered, helping Mrs.Potter straighten up. "Should you not be resting?"

Mrs.Potter did not take her eyes off Tharani but tapped Stanley's arm. "I have never had anybody take care of me the way she did, master Stanley," she said, misty-eyed. "I felt like my mother was looking after me. She fed me, cleaned me, bathed me...."Overwhelmed by emotion, She could speak any further.

"Now, Mrs.Potter. We cannot have you falling sick again." Stanley hugged his nanny. "You should be resting. Lay down. I will take Tharani to our room."

"Oh. Please do not wake her up! She...."

Stanley smiled at Mrs.Potter's concern. "I am not going to wake her up. I will carry her...."

"Are you feeling better, master Stanley?" Mrs. Potter asked. So engrossed was she in her gratefulness to Tharani that Mrs.Potter did not inquire after her master's health.

"I am. It was just a mild fever and an itch." Stanley winked. He bent over Tharani and picked her up gently. Tharani opened her eyes when lifted, but so tired was she that she merely rested her head against his chest and went right back to sleep on seeing that it was Stanley. Carrying her into their room, Stanley kissed her forehead before laying her down. "Sleep well, my love," he whispered in her ear.

23

"Where did the ladies go this time? Stanley asked Pichaiah as the latter began setting lunch for his young master. He was a little disappointed that Tharani did not bring him his lunch. It was not something expected of her. She started it, and he enjoyed having their lunches together. Today was his first time back at the temple site after his sickness. The whole house was being cleaned following their recovery from the illness. Swamy had invited them to stay at his place, but both Tharani and he had declined.

Sitting at home was not something that he enjoyed. The clearing of the temple lake was at its very end. Per a couple of previously written journals, there seemed to be hidden treasures at the bottom of the lake. Stanley did not want to miss out on the discoveries. Early that day, he received a letter from Swamy informing him of the latter's visit to the temple after lunch and a request for Stanley to join them for dinner, along with Tharani and Mrs.Potter.

No longer required to harbor any ill feelings toward his father-in-law, Stanley accepted the invitation with sincerity. Tharani had not been home since they got married. The visit would make her very happy. But where did she go? and when will she return?

"Tharanamma and Mrs.Potter went templu, Stunle babu." Pichaiah said, "Tharanamma wash stepsu for you. "

"Wash steps for me? what do you mean?" Stanley frowned.

"Ammorru saved Potteramma, you. Tharanamma happy. Clean Ammorru temple to Thank you, Ammorru."

It did not make sense to Stanley "How many steps are there?" He asked.

Pichaiah scratched his head. Now, how should he say the number? He flashed both his hands with his ten fingers spread out.

"Ten?" Stanley asked. Pichaiah flashed his fingers again, "twenty?" Pichaiah flashed his fingers another time, "Thirty? Ok! how many tens are there?" he asked. Pichaiah showed both his hands again. Stanley frowned. "A hundred! That woman is mad!" Stanley got to his feet. Pichaiah stalled him and showed two fingers. Stanley's face flushed red "Two hundred?" he said between clenched teeth. Pichaiah nodded, smiling that he was able to get the message across.

"Go back home, Pichaiah. I am going to the temple, " he stormed out.

A couple of hours later, Gowri Devi chided her younger daughter, *"Enough of looking at your husband. Finish your dips in the water and get going. It is already past lunchtime. When will you finish this? When will you and Alludu garu come home."* She asked in a sing-song voice.

"Why are you scolding me? I did not ask him to come. And, how was he to know that he should not touch me? He was trying to save me." despite her logical rationale, Tharani could not help but glare at her husband at the current state of affairs.

At the far end of the temple pond, Stanley stood with Mrs.Potter. What he wanted to happen did not happen; what he wanted to stop continued in an unexpected turn of events.

"Me think you should return to work, master Stanley," Mrs.Potter suggested, almost apologetically. Stanley slapped his cap against his thigh. "This is by far the most ridiculous situation I have ever been in, Mrs.Potter." he complained, "How in hell was I to know that I should not be touching her?! She is doing this. Whatever it is. For us and we are not allowed. Ridiculous is what it is!!"

Mrs.Potter did not think it would be nice on her part to correct him that, she was allowed to stay. It was only Master Stanley that was asked to stay away or instead leave. An elderly couple who had witnessed the incident, on their way into the temple, were walking out, passing by Stanley and Mrs.Potter. Before crossing them, the husband and wife made it a point to share their disapproving looks with Stanley. "She is my wife!" Stanley frowned at the couple. They were not the first or the only ones to have shared their disapproval. *"Naa bhaarya!"* Stanley repeated, pointing towards Tharani. "How long is this going to take?! He asked Mrs.Potter.

"I am not sure, sir. I gathered from Mrs.Wittamore's explanation that it would be another 2-3 hours. She will have to clean and climb all the steps again! Oh, God bless that child! She hasn't even eaten since morning." Mrs.Potter explained, feeling very sorry for Tharani. And, not as much for Stanley.

Stanley looked at Tharani, making her final dip in the temple water. She then walked out of the pond, carrying a big pot of water, making her way toward them. As she crossed them, it was pretty obvious, in the way she looked at him, that he was being held responsible for her predicament. That was it, Stanley decided. No more of his illogical humdrum. Agreed, he was not invited to the temple. But what was wrong with wanting to be part of a ceremony that his wife had promised the goddess? The promise itself did not make any sense to him, not that he was questioning the belief.

She had not asked them to join her at the temple. But, given how she was looked after, Mrs.Potter wanted to accompany Tharani and help in any way that she could. However, when they reached the temple, Gowri Devi made it quite clear that Tharani was to do the work all by herself.

By the time Stanley got to the temple, Tharani was almost halfway up, bending over the steps in the blazing afternoon sun. As he reached her, Mrs.Potter, standing a little further up, noticed him run up the steps and called out to him. What happened then was a rush of incidents leading to the present awkward situation. Hearing Stanley's name, Tharani rose in haste and swooned due to a sudden posture change. Stanley covered the last couple of steps in giant strides, catching her from falling backward. He lifted her into his arms and sat down on a step, holding her in his lap. Gowri Devi immediately sprinkled some cool water on her face while Stanley tapped her gently on the cheek. A moment later, Tharani fluttered her eyes open. "Are you alright, darling?" he asked, holding her up. Tharani nodded. Just when Stanley began to voice his disappointment, a calm voice spoke in Telugu.

"Is she alright?" The priest asked.

"Yes. Yes." Gowri Devi replied, *"She was in the sun all afternoon, right. The heat got to her head."* she said.

The priest leaned to one side to look at Tharani. Seeing him, Tharani hurriedly got off Stanley's lap and walked up to the priest. He was the same priest who had conducted their unusual wedding at the request of Swamy. Naga Ambica Shastry was the fourth-generation chief priest of the temple and the prominent astrological consultant of Swamy's household. For the first time in their association thus

far, Swamy decided to veto Shastry's advice of not
getting the two married. While the priest saw the
marriage as a mishap and a punishment for past sins,
Swamy chose to look at it as divine intervention. 'If
god chose it to happen this way, who are you and me
to rewrite god's will?' was what Swamy had said. *"Do
you want to continue with the task, Tharani amma?"*
he asked.

*"Yes. I will continue. I have already completed more
than 100 steps, sir."* Tharani said.

"Hmm. The thing is, amma." He said, looking at
Gowri Devi. *"Any promise, being fulfilled, for the
goddess, should be done with the utmost discipline,
dedication, and purity of body and mind. "* The priest
explained. *"As you already know."* he rationalized.

"Yes, of course." Gowri Devi replied. Tharani, too,
nodded her head in agreement.

*"Hmm. Given your proximity with your husband just
now, I am sorry to say you will have to restart the
whole process again."* He stated.

*"What? She was fainting, and that is why he held her!
You saw that!"* Gowri Devi protested.

"What I saw is irrelevant." The priest remained calm.
*"If you want to treat it as a chore and finish, it is
between the goddess and you. But, if you are truly
grateful to the goddess for the blessings bestowed,
you must fulfill the promise with devotion. Now I
leave it up to you. Is it your convenience or what the
goddess rightfully deserves?"* He finished.

Tharani felt uneasy at the priest's talk. He seemed to display a certain kind of arrogance that she had never seen him show in the presence of her father. But she also did not want to ridicule the goddess's blessing. Tharani was genuinely grateful for the recovery of Mrs.Potter and Stanley. So, if she had to do it all over again, then so be it. She folded her hands in a namaste and prayed to the goddess. *"Alright. I will do it."* She informed the priest.

Satisfied by his impact, the priest smiled, *"Go to the temple pond and start with a purifying bath."* He said. Both the ladies looked at Stanley, Making their way to the pond. Clueless as he was, Stanley understood Tharani's Telugu. The priest's nasal slang he could not understand. "What? What happened?"

And that was what happened. After a long, tiring time in the afternoon sun, Tharani finally completed her *vratham*. She pressed her sore back with a hand and straightened herself. Never would she make that kind of a promise, Tharani thought to herself. Better yet, she would not let her family fall sick again. She slowly limped towards Mrs. Potter and her husband. Despite the brunt he had to bear for a very unknowing mistake on his part, Stanley stood his ground and did not go away from the temple. There was no way he would leave his wife and go. With nothing much to do and unable to help, Stanley worked himself into a fit by the time Tharani completed her task. The priest, Stanley, ignored. His wife's ignorance enraged him. He always reminded himself that Tharani's promise to the goddess was more of her affection towards him and Mrs.Potter rather than an act of pure lack of rationale. Fear can, after all, paralyze a person and not make them think straight. That thought alone prevented him from doing what he wanted to do. To scream at his wife for this ridiculous situation she created for herself and him.

"Here, child!" Mrs.Potter said, holding out a copper flask, "Have some water. You have turned quite red! Even for your complexion!" she fussed over Tharani. Sitting down on a nearby elevated pavement, Tharani looked at her husband for any reaction. She was, after all, quite proud of what she had done. Stanley, though, had a very different perspective of the situation. His knuckle turned white with the force his hands clenched into fists. His mouth was a thin line of anger, and his face flushed red like an apple. He stared out into the horizon, not trusting himself to keep calm. Mrs.Potter moved away, wanting to talk to Gowri Devi, who was having a conversation with the priest. Seeing her Leave, Tharani reached for Stanley's hand. "Listen?" she started softly. "You eat food?" she asked, taking her hand to her mouth. "Right! Is that what you should be asking me, Tharani?!" Stanley spoke through clenched teeth. He was trying very hard not to break loose. His anger was not what she needed right now. "Did it ever occur to you that such matters should be discussed with me? Your husband! Before you decided to break your

back, climbing up to the temple?!!
Madwoman! *Neeku pichi!*" he said.
Stanley speaking in Telugu was not only un-
understandable, but it was also hilarious. So much so
that his anger did not serve its purpose. Tharani
smiled for the first time all day. "*I am mad, ok. You
are also mad.*" she teased.
"I should be. For letting you do such foolish things."
he shot back rather firmly. Tharani sprang to her feet
and gently slapped him on both his cheeks.
"What...Wha...Stop Tharani!" He grabbed both her
hands. Tharani blushed deeply, looking to either side
to ensure nobody was watching and trying to tug
herself free. "If the priest says one word, I will carry
you away from here!" Stanley warned, pulling her
closer. Tharani tried to tug herself free. "Now.
Promise me you will never do anything stupid like
this again," he said.
Tharani frowned. "It no stupid." she protested.
Stanley pulled her closer, "Promise me." he asked
again.
"It.Not.Stupid!" Tharani persisted. Stanley began to
wrap his arm around her. "No, no, no!! Promise!
Promise!" Tharani hurried out lest anybody witness
her husband's shameful behavior.
Stanley let go of her and smiled contently. "Right.
Shall we go home?" he asked.
Tharani took a couple of steps away from him and
shook her head. "I go home with Amma," she said,

pointing at her mother. "You come home. Nana's home. Dinner. Alright?"

"Not alright." he frowned.

"Why?" she asked, matching his frown.

Hmm. Good question. Why should she not go to her father's place without him? But it was only a matter of some hours, and both of them would go together, right? True. "We are going there for dinner, Tharani. Why do you have to go now?"

"I go with you, amma will say. *Give him this, give him that, See this, see that.*" She replied emotionally. "I no time with amma. Please!" she pleaded.

Stanley looked into the big, sparkling doe eyes and wondered what had happened to him. He shook his head. He was spending way too much time with the ladies. It was softening his mind. he cleared his throat and spoke, in what he thought was his firm tone, "Alright."

In her happiness, Tharani sprang into his arms. Stanley laughed, raising his hand in the air. He looked around for the priest, "Let it be known to one and all. she.." He pointed at Tharani, "threw herself onto me." he announced.

24

"Athamma, please do not go." Stanley followed his mother-in-law into the house. Having spent a fair amount of his recuperating time learning to speak Telugu with the proper pronunciation, Stanley was all out to impress Tharani's family. *"Can I give you a small gift?"* he asked, pulling out a velvet pouch from his pocket.

At the sound of her son-in-law addressing her, Gowri Devi froze in her stance. From the time Stanley came to their house, his attempt to speak in Telugu delighted everybody. Tharani and Swamy would correct him where necessary. For the most part, though, he was doing quite well. Following a scrumptious dinner, Swamy had directed his family into the vast backyard garden. A table and chairs were set out, with sweets and drinks served on a silver platter. The smell of the night queen and the moonlight set a delightful mood. The ladies were seated along the veranda, occasionally joining in on the conversation. Stanley was pleasantly surprised when, on Swamy's asking, Tharani played the Veena. Melodious music, the tunes Stanley had never heard, flowed as Tharani's fingers skillfully plucked at the strings. It was a joyous moment for everybody. When Tharani finished playing, Gowri Devi took her inside the house to ward off *dishti,* any evil eye, on her talented daughter. It was then that Stanley called out to her. Gowri Devi turned around slowly, wondering about the need for her son-in-law to address her directly.

Stanley pulled out a dozen golden bangles studded with rubies from the pouch. *"I bought these for you, Athamma,"* he said.

Gowri Devi smiled. *"Your goodness is gift enough for me, alludugaru. What more can I ask for?"* she said.

"You do not like the bangles?" Stanley asked. He probably should have consulted Swamy before he bought the gift, he wondered. Swamy and Gowri Devi had always been very gracious hosts. Even before he became a member of this house, Stanley wanted to present the couple with tokens of appreciation. Then, unexpectedly the wedding took place, sending his emotions awry. The visit to Hyderabad gave him the clarity that he was seeking. Now was the time to celebrate.

"Ayyo! That is not what I meant." Gowri Devi hurried. She did not want to hurt his feelings, but how could she accept a gift from a son-in-law? She looked at Swamy for help. Stanley followed her gaze. "May I present *Athamma* with a gift, Mr.Swamy?"

"Of course," Swamy replied. He was a content and happy man today. His lord had blessed him with good husbands for his daughters. Through the evening, Swamy noticed the fondness, Tharani felt for Stanley. It shone in her eyes. It was an immense relief that his daughter no longer mourned a lost love. "She is your Athamma. Only, I wish I was your Mamagaru instead of Mr.Swamy," he said.

Stanley laughed, "Of course. Of course." When he turned back to Gowri Devi, she held her hand out. Hmm, now how should he proceed? During his stay, Stanley observed that most people in this region seldom exchanged items in the hands of each other. The items were placed on a nearby surface and were collected by the receiver. But how does one do it with family? He did not want his gesture to offend his mother-in-law. He was about to ask Swamy when Gowri Devi tilted her head in question. Unsure of how to proceed, Stanley gently grabbed her wrist and began slipping the bangles onto her hand. Gowri Devi gasped in surprise before pulling her *pallu* over her mouth to cover her blush. "I am sorry, Athamma. I am not sure of how to give the gift. I hope you forgive my boldness." he smiled sheepishly. Stanley looked towards Tharani and winked. Far from blushing, Tharani winked back at him before sprinting over to her father.

Swamy cleared his throat. "*You ARE quite bold, Alludugaru. You are the only other man to have held* *my wife's han*d," he stated, in mock firmness, before he and Tharani broke into laughter.

" Shoo! Stop your teasing! Shameless people! Should you be laughing at your son-in-law?" Gowri Devi chided. *"Come here."* She grabbed Tharani's hand and hurried out of the room.

With the ladies gone, the men got down to serious talk. Early that evening, Stanley had informed Swamy that he would be leaving for England shortly. "How long will it take for you to reach your land, Alludugaru?" he asked.

"Well, I have booked two cabins on the express. With good weather, we should be home in 5 months or less." Stanley explained.

Swamy was surprised. "Five months is a long time on the sea. " Will there be enough food and facilities?" he asked. Nobody from his family, near or far, had ever traveled by sea. It was a territory he was unfamiliar with; hence, he was very unsure. "Two rooms would be enough?"

Stanley smiled. "The rooms are for us, Mr.Swamy. We have cargo allowance with the rooms we have booked," he explained.

"Oh," Swamy said thoughtfully. Before speaking again, he folded his hands in a namaste and addressed Stanley. "This will be the first time Tharani is stepping into your family home." he hesitated before continuing, "I know that you do not like to receive gifts from us. But, I cannot send my daughter with bare hands from my house to yours. Please." Swamy requested, "Please allow me to send some good wishes to your family." he asked.

Stanley felt terrible for how he had treated Swamy at his wedding. Unknowing as it may have been, he could have, at the least, been more polite about it. "You embarrass me with your humility, sir." he said, "Please accept apologies for my uncivil behavior,"

"I do not understand, Alludugaru," Swamy said. Stanley spent the next few minutes explaining why he behaved the way he did and his newly acquired information about who was to blame. "No. No." Swamy shook his head and bowed it. "Please forgive me on behalf of my brother-in-law. He should not have done what he did." Swamy announced. At the same time, the ladies walked back into the room.

"The ladies need not be aware of this, Sir. Your daughter could have held me to gunpoint for treating you so poorly." Stanley quipped.

Swamy smiled. "I am sorry to say that she got that from her mother. Both of them are very protective of us. Prabhavathi is like me. She is a good girl."

"Are you telling my husband I am not good?" Asked Tharani.

"I am telling him that you are a monkey. He should tie you to the bedpost to stop your mischief." Swamy teased.

Tharani slipped a little behind Stanley and held his arm. *"He will not do anything like that,"* she pouted. She looked at him for confirmation.

Stanley tapped her hand, "I would not wish to, my dear. Although I believe I should follow his advice when you do not listen to me." He teased.

Tharani gasped at his statement, *"Amma!"* She ran back to her mother.

"Oh. Stop teasing the girl. She had a hard day!" Gowri Devi admonished her husband.

Swamy laughed. *"Well, A few months, and she will no longer be with us. Then who will tease her?"* he said, leaning towards his daughter.

"What?!" Gowri Devi and Tharani asked at the same time.

"Ahh. I did not get a chance to discuss it with you since I returned. We are leaving for England in four weeks. I..."

"You go." Tharani huffed, leaving Stanley's side and moving to her father.

"WE are going, Tharani," Stanley said firmly, knowing that an argument would ensue.

"No..." Tharani started when Swamy interrupted.

"Ranamma." he said gently, *"You can run your own house, as Amma does. Do you understand?"*

Tharani began to shake her head vehemently. *"I am not going. I am not going,"* she said to Stanley. *"You stay here,"* she told him.

He probably should have explained to her in private, Stanley thought. Then again, having her parents calm her down did not seem like a bad idea. "We will leave in four weeks, Tharani. You still have time with your

parents. We WILL be leaving, though. You have to take your place as Mrs.Wittamore." he said.
"No! I do not go. You go." Tharani said.
"We shall discuss this after going home," Stanley said. He did not want to argue at his in-law's house.
"Please stay back for the evening, Alludugaru!" Swamy requested.
"I am afraid I will have to decline. Mrs.Porter has not been keeping well since her outing in the afternoon sun today and hence, could not accept your invitation. I do not want to leave her all alone. " Stanley explained. He leaned a little to the side to look at Tharani. "Shall we take our leave, my dear?" he asked. Tharani twisted her lips to the side and turned her back to him. "Tharani?"
"Can she stay for two days?" Gowri Devi asked Stanley, though she looked at her husband. *"That is big news for her to digest. I will make her understand. She will be more agreeable then."* she requested.
For the second time that day, a request was made that Stanley did not want to oblige. He almost denied it when Gowri Devi looked at him. Now he knew where the Tharani got her eyes! If looks could kill, the ladies in this family were soft murderers. In sharp contrast to his slightly shaking head, Stanley replied, "Of course." he smiled reluctantly. After an exchange of appreciation and apologies, he made his way to the stable. Swamy and Gowri Devi let the couple walk out alone. "So, you are not coming home," Stanley stated.

"You not staying," Tharani stated, too.

"Hmm. How long will you stay?"

"Two days. You come to take me?" Tharani asked.

"No," Stanley replied. "You come back on your own."

Tharani frowned. "You angry? Why? You tell me come to your home, far. I not like to come. I still talk nice to you. Why you angry with me?" she questioned.

"You..." Stanley leaned closer to her face, "my darling, do not have a choice about coming to England. That is my home. And, as my wife, it is now your home, too.

Tharani curled her toes. There! There was that feeling again! Her stomach always fluttered when he came that close to her. Trying not to look embarrassed, she tilted her nose, "*I will see.*"

"*Nothing to see.* I will carry you over my shoulder if I have to. *Ardhamayinda?*" He shook his head the Indian way.

Tharani smiled. *"Understood. Understood."* She shook her head like a doll.

"Good. Now go into the house before I change my mind about letting you stay."

25

Stanley slapped his hat across his leg as he watched
Varaha Swamy. The boy and his friends napped on a
tree trunk overlooking the river bank. He was
confronting his brother-in-law about a personal matter
for the second time. The first one was a coincidence,
so that would not count. What else was Stanley to do?
Tharani had said she would come back in two days. It
was now two weeks since she stayed back at her
parents' house. Yet, there was no sight of her coming
back. Stanley did receive a letter every morning. The
eagerness to read the letter lasted only as long as he
opened it, for she wrote in Telugu. He could not read
them, nor could he have somebody else read a private
correspondence from his wife. What was she
thinking?! The first week, he let be, seeing as he was
busy with all the preparations for the departure and
that he had told Tharani that she was to come back by
herself.
Despite his stance and his ego, he had, one day, made
his way toward Swamy's house. Only to have Varaha

meet him halfway and inform him that Tharani and his mother were visiting his uncle and aunt in the next town. Hmm. Upset as he was, Stanley had to reason with himself. After all, it might be a few years before Tharani would see her family and friends again. But did she not miss him? Did she not want to see him, even once in the past two weeks? That thought angered him more than his rationale allowed. Was he the more affected in this relationship? He took in a deep breath and approached Varaha.

"Junior Swamy!" he called out with a smile.

The voice of his fair brother-in-law almost tripped Varaha over the trunk and into the river. His friend held and steadied him. To Stanley's surprise, Varaha looked agitated rather than his usual stoic self.

"Ba..bawagaru!" Varaha stuttered, "I..."

Stanley frowned. What was wrong with this boy? Why did he become pale? "You what, Junior?" Stanley asked, not realizing that he was still frowning. Seeing his brother-in-law's face, Varaha became even more ashamed. "I...I.I am very sorry. *My friends wanted to see you, and I did. I did not know how to ask you. Naanagaru said that it would not be nice. But my friends. My friends insisted. So.."*

"So?" Stanley teased.

"We were there for a very short time, bawagaru. Promise!" Varaha placed a hand over his head. "*I did not let them stay. They...They just wanted to see you. I took them away as soon as they saw you from the*

window. Promise!" Varaha began to sweat. "Please.
Please do not tell Naanagaru." he pleaded.
Stanley continued to frown and looked over Varaha's
shoulder at his friends, huddled together. "That was
not a very nice thing to do, Junior Swamy. That is no
way to behave at your sister's house."
"I am sorry." Varaha hung his head.
Stanley smiled. "You should have brought your
friends inside the house to meet me. How about this?
I invite You and your friends for the evening supper
at my home today." He looked at his friends and
repeated the same in Telugu. The boys bounced with
joy.
His mission accomplished, Stanley went about his
work. In the evening, Varaha and his friends dressed
in their silkiest best to impress the fair-skinned
brother-in-law. Stanley treated them to a very English
meal of soups, loaves of bread, bird meat, and
pudding. All to the credit of a very happy-to-indulge
Mrs.Potter. Throughout the evening, Varaha
answered all the questions Stanley asked, with
additional input from his friends. "And she will be
there?" He asked.
"Yes! Amma said that she should practice every day.
But Akka does not listen. If Amma is not there, Akka
only plays with her feet in the water."
"Does she?" Stanley was not surprised. "Hmm. Are
you certain it will not be a problem?" he asked.

"Of course not, Bawagaru," Varaha confirmed, taking a sip of the soup. "You are the *Alludu* of our family," he said.

Stanley smiled at the boy, "Right."

The following day was not as pleasant for Varaha, for teaching his older sister to swim was not a task he enjoyed. "*But, Akka, we float better in deeper waters! How else will you learn to swim?*" He was exasperated.

"*When I don't know how to swim, how do you expect me to jump into the river?!*" Tharani asked, not understanding the logic.

Varaha had had enough. He turned to his mother, "*Amma! I am not teaching her anymore! She will never learn.*" he complained. "*Tomorrow, if the ship sinks, then don't blame....*"

"*Shut up, Varaha!*" Gowri Devi scolded, "*What are those unpleasant words! Are you trying to scare your sister? If you are not good enough to teach her to swim, then what is the use of your talent?*" She asked Varaha before turning her glare on Tharani. "*And you, girl?! How will you protect yourself if something happens to the ship? What if your husband is not near you at the time?*" she asked in a matter-of-fact voice.

"*Amma.....*" Tharani started.

"*No, Amma. No gimma.* " Gowri chided. " In a reminiscing tone, she continued. "*The day your father and I got married, we were crossing the river when our boat turned over. Everybody fell into the water. Thank god your father was a good swimmer. He pulled me out of the water. Otherwise, I would have been washed away, like your father's great aunt. You kids would not have existed. Do you know how many people said how many things to me for how many days?!* " She said, still tearing up at the agony she had to endure during her marriage's early days. *"How can I be blamed for the heavy rains? Or for the overcrowded boat? Still, everybody blamed me. All that happened because your father married me, it seems! If your father were not as good as he is, I would have left the house and gone."* she stated. *"I, though, just crossed a river. You are crossing; god knows how many seas. You must know how to swim. Do you understand?"*

"I understand, Amma! Why is Naana not here? He teaches nicely. This fellow..." Tharani pointed at her brother,*" he just yells at me...."*

"You are not listening...." Varaha began before his mother cut him off.

"Will both of you stop it? Kanna, have some patience. In the little time she is here, you want to fight with her?" she asked and then turned to Tharani. *"Your father would have taught you if he did not decide to buy everything from every corner of this world to send to your in-law's house. Now, stop irritating your brother and get into the water. You are going to have our noses chopped! Hardly two weeks left! And there is so much for you to learn. There is so much for me to do! God only knows what kind of ......"* she turned around to walk away when she saw Stanley quietly

walk towards them. He folded his hands in a silent namaste and immediately put a finger to his lips, asking his mother-in-law not to speak.

Tharani huffed and looked at the water. *"Why will I behave like this at my in-laws' house? I know you will not believe me, but I will not let anybody say anything to naana."* she stated, *"Did I say that I will not learn to swim? Just that the water is so deep? What if I don't float?"*

"What if you swim?" Stanley spoke in her ear. Tharani jerked around, startled at his voice.

"You?" she asked in startled surprise.

"Who else?" Stanley looked into her eyes. Though he smiled, his eyes held a stronger emotion. Almost arrogant. Not giving her time to respond, Stanley lifted her into his arms. "Hold on tight," he said before jumping over the edge straight into the water. Gowri Devi and Varaha peeked over. Once Stanley and Tharani resurfaced, Gowri Devi took Varaha's hand and led him away.

"What about Akka and Ba...."

"They will be fine. Just keep quiet and come." Gowri Devi smiled at her son-in-law's naughtiness.

Inside the water, Stanley let go of Tharani and waited for her to reach the surface. Tharani struggled and spluttered, *"Hold m...hold...hold me."* She tried to call out.

"Here." Stanley extended a hand towards her. "Hold on. Try to peddle your legs." Tharani held his hand with both of hers and tried moving closer. "Oh, no, no. Stay afloat."

Tharani managed to hold herself up. "Why you do that?" She asked.

"How else will you learn?" He asked.

"I got scared, you know. You pick me and jump." Stanley began swimming towards the bank, with Tharani holding on. "Well, I suppose it serves you right to get scared." He spoke arrogantly.

Tharani stalled him. He had never spoken to her in such a manner. Why now? Was he not as happy as her to see each other again? "You angry?" She asked. Stanley jerked her closer to him and held her by the waist. "It was supposed to be two days, Tharani! Two days!" He whispered close to her face. Tharani frowned, not understanding the meaning "it has been two weeks now. Did you not want to come back?" he asked. The question and the emotion were on two completely different planes. Tharani opened her mouth to answer. Stanley promptly shut it with his. He leaned back against the muddy ledge and pulled Tharani onto his thighs. His hand massaged her neck while his tongue flirted with hers. When she moaned and wrapped her hands around his neck, he pulled back in a gasp. "So, you do not want to come back? He asked. The question did not register in Tharani's dazed mind. Again, Stanley did not let her answer. He leaned in closer and gently bit her lip. *"No answer?"* he asked before closing his lips on hers. He waited for her to lean in on him and slowly lowered his hand to her bottom, pushing her closer to his desire. At the sudden feel of his manhood, Tharani tried to move away. Stanley persisted. His hold was firm, and his movement persuasive. He used both hands to nudge her closer and felt smug when Tharani did not pull away from their kiss. Now was the time, he thought. He turned around, holding Tharani against the muddy ledge. He deepened the kiss one last time and, to Tharani's shock, pulled away entirely from her. He held her long enough to stop her from dropping down. "Right!" he said, catching his breath. "You do not want to come back?" he spoke, striding back into the water. "Don't," he commanded, jumped back into the water, and swam away from her. Tharani shuddered at the cool air against her warm and flushed body. What just happened? What did he do? And why was he leaving? Still feeling unsteady and unsure of the rush of emotions she felt, Tharani called out to Stanley, "Listen!!"

"I will not!" Stanley shouted back. Reaching the other side of the river bank, he did not turn around to look at her and began walking away. Now, she would come back! He had not lost his sensual touch and was proud of it.

26

And she did come! Not the same evening, though. Or the next. Or the day after. Stanley stared beyond Tharani, looking at everything but her.

He looked at the trunks unloaded from the bullock carts—the pots, filled with sweet delicacies, placed in the open central yard of his house.

He also looked at his young brother-in-law, standing in front of him with a sweet apologetic smile. He looked at everything except his beautiful wife and her mesmerizing doe eyes. Tharani tried to catch his gaze with every possible, subtle gesture she could manage in front of all the people bringing the gifts her mother had sent along. But Stanley was not ready to budge. If she did not care for him enough to come back the same day, he had next to nothing to say to her. Coming around the same evening as the day he left her trembling in the river was probably a bit much to expect. But showing up a full three days after was utterly unacceptable. Did she have any idea of the kind of questions it raised about a man's confidence in himself?!! Did she?! Obviously, not! Then, why should he care?

"Is this all, or do I have to book an extra berth, junior Swamy?" Stanley asked.

Varaha smiled shyly. "Amma said that Nana would arrange for the rest to be brought to the ship, Bawagaru. She also said sorry because Nanna could not come in time to bring Akka here himself. He is still in the northern town." he explained Swamy's absence for the past couple of weeks.

"Then I do have to book another berth," Stanley said. From the corner of his eye, he noticed Tharani move away to meet Mrs.Potter. "Right, then. Shall I accompany you halfway through? He asked.

"I am not going home, Bawagaru. I must go to my uncle's house in the next village." Varaha said and took leave.

"Mrs. Potter, I will not be coming home for supper. Do not wait up for me." Stanley said, walking out the door.

Anklets jingled behind him. "Listen!" he heard. And ignored.

There was not much work at the temple site to keep him busy. The final bits of excavation were handed over to the temple architect. Much as he wanted to stay back to see the whole temple complex, Stanley had to leave to take up his long-ignored position at Whittamore. He sat over the edge of the temple pond and sketched the outline in his small, personal pocket journal. When the afternoon sun reached overhead,

Stanley made his way to the makeshift desk under the tree. Halfway up, he saw Tharani waiting under the tree. A carrier of food was on the desk. A sight that would have, under normal circumstances, brought a smile to his face. Today, though, he felt completely different about it. He was upset with Tharani and wanted her to know that. So, he chose to look the other way and walk away, even after she saw and waved at him.

He waited out the entire afternoon in a deeper portion of the complex and did not come out till it was time for the men to leave for the day. Even then, he did not go back home. He made his way to the wrestling camp and elbowed out his frustration. He then went for a long swim in the river's calm waters. On his way home, he spoke to every person he knew and shared a word or smile. He finally reached home when the moon was high and bright in the dark sky.

Stanley noticed a faint light from his study windows as he approached his house. He frowned. Was she waiting for him? Or did she forget to turn off the lamp? He walked up the steps and made to knock on the door. The door opened gently before Stanley's fist landed on it.

"Why you late?!" Tharani asked, slightly miffed.

Oh! She is mad at him?! Stanley frowned deeper than Tharani. "You can answer that yourself." He said through tight lips.

"What?" Tharani asked, not understanding the question.

"Move out of the way, Tharani," he said. Without waiting for a response, he pushed her arm and walked into the house. Tharani closed the door and sprinted after him into the study.

"You not talk to me?" she asked, coming up behind him. When he did not respond and continued to look at his desk, she grabbed his arm and nudged him to turn around.

"What do you want, Tharani!" he hissed and regretted it immediately as her eyes welled with tears.

Hurt as she was by his behavior, Tharani did not want to cry. She batted her eyelids to keep the tears from flowing out. "Why..." she choked. "Why you.."

Stanley ran his fingers through his hair. "Leave me alone for some time, Tharani. I am a little tired and have work to do. We can talk later." he sat down at his desk and pulled out his pocket journal. Tharani stood looking at his back. Only one question in her mind. Why was he behaving this way? When, even after five minutes, he did not turn around to acknowledge his presence, she ran out of the room, letting the tears flow out. After a moment, Stanley smacked his pen on the desk. What was he doing?! He did not even let her speak. Nor gave her the time and opportunity. What got into him? Sighing, he made his way to his bedroom. Only to find it empty. Where did she go? He walked into the central yard and looked around. She was nowhere. A cool draft of wind made him turn towards the backyard. The door was open.

Where the hell did she go?!! He ran out in a fit of
fear, straight towards the stable. God, help him. How
far did that woman go?! He mounted his horse and
strode towards the exit.

"I am here!" Tharani called out just as Stanley was
about to leap onto the street. She was sitting on the
'*ghattu,*' elevated platforms on either side of
doorways that allowed people to sit in for
conversations. Dangling her feet over the edge, she
stared at him with anger and sadness.

Stanley closed his eyes and took a deep breath,
reigning in anger and the horse. "You could not speak
up before I mounted the horse?" he asked, trying not
to shout at her.

"You not want to talk to me," Tharani said sadly,
staring straight into his eyes.

That sadness upset Stanley. He did not get off the
horse. Instead, he reached out his hand, "Come here."
he said.

Tharani looked at his hand. She wanted to refuse. At
the same time, she did not like this conflict between
them. Her mother's words rang in her mind. *Never go
to sleep without resolving a fight.* She walked up to
the horse. Stanley pulled her up in front of him. He
looked up at the sky. The full moon made everything
shine silver.

"Have you seen the waterfall on a full moon night?"
he asked. Tharani shook her head in response. "Shall
we go see?" He nudged the horse into a canter.

"*First, tell me why you are angry,*" Tharani asked, expressing her anguish fluently in Telugu rather than stuttering in English.

Stanley, too, decided to speak fluently.

"I am not angry, Tharani. I am merely upset."

Tharani frowned. "Angry. Upset. *What is the difference?*"

Well, how does one explain an emotion without inviting more questions? Stanley moved Tharani's braid to one side and nipped at her ear with his teeth. Tharani shrugged and jerked her head away. "That is upset." He said, without showing any emotion. "Do you want me to continue?" He asked. Unsure of what to expect, Tharani frowned but turned her back to him again. Stanley lowered his head to the base of her neck. He nuzzled for a few seconds before taking a bite of her shoulder and gently massaging it between his teeth. His tongue tickled. The pressure of his teeth gradually increased till pleasure rolled into pain. Tharani's gentle gasp changed into a sudden wince. Instead of jerking away, she tapped hard on his hand. "Stop!!". Stanley let go. Even in the glow of the moonlight, he could see the marks his teeth had left. "That, my dear, is anger." He stated. Tharani rubbed her shoulder, maintaining silence. Neither she nor Stanley spoke a word till they reached the falls.

As they strode through the trees, the sound of the falling waters boomed in the air. Tharani had never been out this late in the night. The trees opened up to the upper half of the waterfalls. She stared in awe at the scene in front of her eyes.

The gentle stream rolled over the cliff's edge into a roaring fall. The full moon loomed large on the horizon in the clear starlit sky. Stanley dismounted and lifted Tharani down. He walked his horse to a tree, where the grass was lush, and tethered it as he patted down the horse's neck.

Tharani walked to a tree away from him and stood in silence, waiting for him to turn around. "*Amma did not let me come.*" She said to his back. When Stanley did not respond, she continued, "*Truly! I told her I wanted to come back home. First she said it was too late. Then she said it was not a good day. Then said it was a Friday. What could I have done?*" she cried. "*She....she even called me shameless!*"

Stanley paused for a moment and then focused utterly on rubbing down the horse. Tharani pouted. Why was he doing this? She knew why, of course. But. How long will he be like this? She did not like it when he did not speak to her. She cannot deny that her behavior was any different during the early days of their marriage, but that did not stop him from talking to her. Why now? Hmm. Tharani thought. Her husband had not shown any ego about talking to her when she was angry with him. Then, why should she get miffed just because he was upset? Tharani rubbed her shoulder, where she could feel the soft dents caused by his teeth. Feeling a tingle in her stomach, she went to him and reached for his hand. "You not talk to me? She asked, turning him around.

With large, appealing eyes staring at him, Stanley found his resolve cracking. Stay strong! He affirmed. "*Sare*, When you talk?"

Pulling his hand away, Stanley answered, "Eventually."

"What?"

Stanley sighed. What was he doing? He cannot be this way. It was difficult trying to stay upset, seeing her efforts to appease him. But..."We can talk later."

"If you talk later, why bring here?" She asked.

Stanley raised his brows. "Good question." He stated. Then remembering what she said earlier, he cleared his throat. "First, You tell me why Attamma called you shameless?" He asked.

Her cheeks flushed as Tharani regretted the slip. "*That...That. I .*" She swallowed and tried looking away from him. *I wanted to come back the same, the same day*."

"Which day?" Stanley asked quite innocently. He knew very well. But, he admitted to himself, this sweet agony of his wife was delightful.

Tharani understood he was teasing her."You not know which day?" She countered.

"No." He shrugged.

Tharani lowered her head and looked at him from under her brows. *"You truly don't remember?"* she asked again. Stanley shook his head. *"Fine then. If you don't remember, then I don't need to remind you."* Saying, she looked away.

Her open neck was an invitation Stanley chose not to decline. He lowered his head, "Ah! You mean the day I did this?" He kissed her neck, holding her against himself.

Tharani held onto his shoulders.

"Listen!" Tharani whispered in a quiver, burying her head into his chest, "Ple.....hmmm." Stanley silenced her with a kiss. He tugged at her saree over her shoulder, low enough to expose part of her breast. Tharani tried to move away in shock at the sudden disrobing. "No!" She gasped loudly.

"Why?" Stanley did not let go.

"You...you see...everything," she said shyly.

He smiled, "Well, you are welcome to see everything of me." He caressed her back, inching the cloth away.

"Please!" She pleaded, too shy to look into his eyes. Suddenly, she was lifted off her feet. *"What are you doing?!"* Tharani asked, seeing that they were heading into the moonlit river.

"I.." Stanley adjusted Tharani's weight in his arms, trying not to lose balance on the rocky bottom "...am finding a solution to your shyness, darling." He stopped when the water was up to his waist. He first lowered her feet into the water. "The water is not too cold. Is that alright?" He asked, gently dropping her. Her husband surprised her. She watched as he took his shirt off and bent over to pull his pants. He tossed his clothes on a nearby rock. "Now, you turn, my dear." He said, sealing her lips with his. He engaged in foreplay with his tongue.

Moaning to the desires that he evoked, Tharani realized that Stanley had worked her clothes off her when she felt his hand on her bare bottom. The next thing she knew, her naked body was flush against his. He lifted her while biting down on her lips. Tharani's body and mind were rocked with conflicting emotions. She was scared that she was doing something she should not be doing. Yet, the feeling that Stanley's hands were arousing was too exciting to withdraw from. His fingers touched and explored intimate parts of her body, which she never knew could be felt that way. A sense of urgency took over her body, wanting to move close to him and run away simultaneously. The heat from his body was becoming too hot to handle. Was it even possible to sweat when you were in the water?!

"I...I...*god!!! You.you.*close.clo..." Tharani could not get any coherent words out of her mouth. She wanted him closer, if that was even possible. Stanley picked her up and held her legs against his waist. He began to walk, holding her, giving her time to catch her breath. Reaching the rock, he grabbed their wet clothes and bundled them together before gently pushing Tharani's back onto them.

He caressed her till she eased against his intrusion and whimpered in pleasure. "It might hurt in the beginning," he warned as he steadied her hips and thrust into her. Tharani bit her lip in pain. She pushed against his chest and squeezed her thighs into him. "Shhhh. Relax darling. It will ease." He pinned her hands on the rock and moved deep and slow until they moved as one. Tharani closed her eyes, enjoying the rhythm of their movement. Stanley's thrusts became faster and more forceful, making Tharani moan louder. The rush she felt was unlike any happiness or agony she had ever experienced. How was that even possible? To feel pleasure and pain at the same time? By the time Stanley found his release, Tharani was limp with ecstasy.

It was long before they could bring themselves to move and ride back home. The excitement of becoming man and wife eluded sleep, despite their well-worked bodies. Stanley lit the lamp on his bedside table and pulled out a bunch of letters from the drawer. He handed them to Tharani. "Now, my dear," he said, "I want to hear all about what you have written."

"All?" She asked, looking fondly at the letters she had written to him when staying at her father's place. He had tied them into a neat little bundle. Stanley nodded. "Ok. First." She held her hand out to him, "My gift."

Stanley frowned. "What gift?" Her utter confidence made him smile. "How do you know that I bought you one?" He asked.

"You gave amma bangles?" She asked.

"Yes, I did."

"Why?"

"Because I like her and..."
Tharani smiled. "You like me more!" She said, proud at her analysis.
Stanley laughed. How very true!!

27

As the departure date to England arrived, Tharani's excitement grew by the hour. Mrs.Potter and Stanley told her fascinating tales of the small nation with the big throne. Everything was something to be in awe of, from the land to the people and their stories. The sadness of having to leave her parents and her land, though frequent, was often overridden by curiosity and fascination for the new and unknown.

"Potter amma told me that everybody goes to the city in the summer and stays there till winter. They meet at each others' houses and dance." Then in a hushed whisper, she said, *"Husbands hold their wives in their arms and dance, it seems, Amma."*

"Mm, Hmm," Gowri Devi smiled at her daughter's excitement. It also worried her. Oh, how was she to live without her?! Tharani and Varaha were the only people in the house who spoke about everything and anything. While Varaha did so by virtue of his age and having to accompany his father, Tharani did it out of sheer excitement of life. She marveled at anything

new. Never afraid of what she did not know, Tharani never lost her childlike enthusiasm for discovering life. But will her in-laws mistake her excitement for silliness? In today's world, a man's enthusiasm was to be encouraged while a woman's excitement was considered vulgar. *"Listen, Tharani, "* Gowri Devi warned as she combed her daughter's long hair gently. *"I know you are excited about going to your husband's home. You also love to talk. "* Tharani interrupted, *"Is it wrong?"* *"No. It isn't. Since you were born and raised here, we know why you speak the way you do. But, your attamma's family will not know that. Often, women who talk a lot are looked down upon. Even called stupid at times. Do you understand? At your attamma's house, don't go on and on like a wedding drum beat. Words and money are precious and should be used sparingly. Are you listening? You should only speak when and as much is needed. The fewer words you use to convey your message, the more value those words will have. You will have. "* she emphasized.

Catering to the needs of a high society house was not new to Tharani. The catch was that everything about her husband's family, home, and the country was new and unknown. Not sure of what hardships her daughter might face, Gowri Devi decided that familiarizing oneself with fundamental human nature was the way to face the unknown.

"Remember," Gowri Devi said as she carefully wrapped bronze statues of *Ganapathy* and Durga *Devi* in a satin cloth and placed them in a carved wooden box. *"People are the same everywhere. God is also the same everywhere. We speak a different language, so we call god by different names. There is nothing wrong with worshipping their god. After all, their god blessed them with the same health and wealth we would have prayed for. Praying to your husband's god is not wrong. Forgetting the blessing that our god has given us is a sin. Do you understand? Find a nice little quiet room on the east side of the house and set up the god's room there. Don't forget to ask your mother-in-law for advice before you set up the room. Did you hear me? She should not feel that you are making changes without consulting her."*

"But she won't know our rituals, na amma."

"But she knows her house, right? She is the mistress of that house. So, anything and everything you should ask her before doing it. But that does not mean you irritate her with questions all day long. Observe what she is doing and follow. If you have questions and feel she might not respond, ask alludu garu first. If he does not know, then ask your mother-in-law. He also has sisters, right?"

"What if none of them know?"

Tharani got knuckled on the head by her mother.

"Then break a coconut on your head. If that gives you some sense, do what it tells you! Silly girl! Here, I am

dying thinking how and what you will do there, and my worry is funny for you?"

Seeing that her mother was more worried about the journey than her, Tharani decided to lighten the mood.

"I AM listening to what you are saying, Amma. I was also terrified, but then naana told me we should not be scared of what we do not know. We should be curious, it seems."

"If men had to do half the work a woman does to run a household, their curiosity would jump in a well! Words are good to listen to. But actions are important. Do you understand?"

"Yes, amma."

"Now." Gowri Dev continued, bending over to open a vast metal trunk filled with the finest silks from local and neighboring weavers. *"In here are clothes for the ladies. I do not know what kind of colors your mother-in-law wears. Your father tried to ask your husband, but he would not answer properly. So, I chose some darker colors for her. The plain and dark-colored silks are for you, Attamma. On this side, all these bright, colorful clothes are for your husband's sisters. I ordered extra wide clothes, so they can be made into those gowns or whatever they choose. But, when you first give them, I wrapped three sarees, each in these clothes, and wrote Attamma and Adapaduchu inside."* Gowri Devi opened the cloth and showed the names she had written down, stating Mother-in-law and sisters-in-

law. *"Give these sarees to them and let them choose the clothes for themselves."*

" *Amma. Enough.*" Tharani stood up and held her stomach. *"All this preparation is making me hungry."*

"Yes. Yes. First, you eat. Come, I made your favorite Pappu charu and Kodi koora."

Gowri Devi's nervousness made her give a discourse, about marital life and the duties of a wife, at any time that she could squeeze in a word or two. Gowri Devi wanted Tharani to be prepared for the life she was stepping into without her parents being able to reach her at any time she needed them. Not knowing what Tharani's in-laws were like, their customs, ritual, and expectations? Much as she wanted her daughter to be prepared for the unknown, mistakes were bound to happen, and they may result in chaos. Was Tharani ready to handle that? Careful as she wanted her daughter to be, she did not wish Tharani to lose herself and her identity of being the young and adventurous kid she was. At the same time, Tharani should be able to conform to the rules of her in-laws' house in order to develop a beautiful relationship with her husband.

"To compromise is not about losing yourself. It means to accept the other person for who they are and continue to nurture your relationship. You do not have to agree with everything your husband is saying. But that also does not mean you contradict him. Try to understand why he is saying what he is saying. Ask questions if you do not understand. But never argue

in front of others and never disrespect each other in front of others. Do you understand?" Gowri Devi had said.

"I don't understand, amma." A confused Tharani replied.

Gowri Devi sat her daughter down. *"When you go there, the only person you know and who knows you and the people over there is your husband. Do you understand? It means that you should listen carefully to what he says and do what he asks you to do. He is not only your husband. He is also you friend and your teacher. Alludugaru likes you, Tharani. You should use that to your advantage. But that also does not mean that you take advantage."*

"I thought I understood what you were saying. Now, again I don't. You are telling me to take advantage and not take advantage, Amma!" Tharani cried.

"Silly girl, listen properly. He likes you, which means that he will do things for you. That also means that you should respect him and not have him play to your tunes. Do you understand? If you want him to keep loving you, that will not happen with bad behavior."

"So you are saying that I should listen to everything he says? Obey him?"

"Obey him, yes. Follow him blindly? No. Men think differently from us women. Men are not always as aware of a house's workings as a woman. And, as his wife, you should guide him to make the right choices that are good for your family. I did not understand your husband's position, but your father tells me he

has a very good social standing. As his wife, it is your responsibility to ensure that you do not do anything that will raise fingers at his choice of bride. Remember, people will judge us based on how you behave. No. Don't interrupt me." Gowri Devi raised a hand when Tharani tried to speak. *"Listen carefully. When a girl gets married and goes to her in-laws' place, misunderstandings are bound to happen. People will talk. Some people will like you, and some people won't. As long as you are doing what your duty is and what is right, people will eventually begin to like you. So whatever they say should not be taken to heart. It also means that you should make all effort to learn what needs to be done. It is better to ask how you are supposed to do things rather than do them wrong. Are you listening to me?"* Gowri Devi continued when Tharani nodded her head. *"And, till you find someone else to help you, your husband is your main reference. Ask him whatever you want. Be honest with him. Take care of him. Make sure he has good food to eat and a peaceful house to sleep in. Never complain about what is wrong. Ask him for suggestions on how to do the right things. Do you understand what I am saying?"*

Tharani yawned. *"You are telling me too many things at the same time, amma."*

"If you were here, you could have written to me with any questions you had. But, with alludugaru being from another country, this Ugadi's question will get you an answer by the time of the next Ugadi." Gowri

Devi went into deep thought. *"May be I should write down some instructions for you. What do you say?"* She asked earnestly.

Tharani nodded her head vigorously. *"Yes! Write! At least I can see your writing, if not you."* Tears welled up in Tharani's eyes. *"Why do I have to go, Amma?! I am very scared."* She cried. *"What if they don't like me? What if I do something wrong and he gets very angry at me? What if I don't want to stay there? What if I want to come back? What if all the girls there are as fair as him, and after seeing them again, he regrets marrying a dark girl like me?!"*

Gowri Devi became all teary-eyed and hugged her daughter when Tharani began her charade. But, at the last question, she pulled her daughter away and hit her on the head. *"What mad stuff are you saying? What is wrong with you? Whoever thinks you are not beautiful just because you are dark is mad, and you don't have to take anything they say seriously. Do you understand? Nobody. Nobody can make you feel less beautiful than yourself just because they are fair. It does not make them beautiful. Do you understand? You are just a shade darker than him. For that itself you become unattractive? Mad girl!!"* She scolded.

For all the jitters his wife was feeling, Swamy was confident of his son-in-law. "I do not doubt your ability to take care of Tharani, alludu garu." He stated calmly, "I only request that you forgive her for any mistakes that she might unknowingly commit. She speaks her mind, and sometimes that is not at the *most appropriate of times."* Swamy held Stanley's hand after a handshake. "She is stubborn, but she listens alludu garu. Please guide her, and you will see that she will make a very good wife."

"You need not assure me of Tharani's obedience as a wife, Mr.Swamy." Stanley laughed and winked in Tharani's direction. Only the five of them had traveled to the port city in Kerala. Stanley could understand the nervousness the parents must feel about having their daughter travel to an unknown land halfway across the globe. Gowri Devi's tension was quite palpable. Despite the language barrier they shared, his mother-in-law had managed to convey to Mrs.Potter, that Tharani was being left in her care. Stanley shook Swamy's hand again. "I hope I stay true to your confidence in me, sir."

To his daughter, Swamy had but a few words *"Take care Rannamma. Don't forget us."* he teased *"Remember, you can write to us about anything you want. OK? Anything."*

Gowri Devi rolled her eyes at Swamy's short dialogue with their daughter. The luggage was loaded into the ship. After Swamy himself inspected the cabins booked for the journey and gave a satisfactory report to his wife, they disembarked the ship, leaving Stanley, Tharani, and Mrs.Potter aboard. As the ship moved away from the shores, Gowri Devi buried her head into her husband's back and cried.

"Shh, Gowri. Tharani can still see us. See, she is still waving. Wave back to her." Swamy pulled Gowri Devi forward.

Sniffling into her sari, Gowri waved back at the receding ship. *"You have to follow her,"* she said unexpectedly, between her sobs.

"What?!"

"You heard me right. You have to follow her. You have to go to their land. Make sure she is settled in properly. Make sure that Alludu garu's house is comfortable for your daughter."

"Have you gone mad?!" Swamy frowned. *"They are not living in the next village, Gowri. He stays on the other side of the planet!"*

"Other side of the planet or the other side of the moon, I don't care!" Gowri Devi cried, *"They say that one has to look at seven generations of the family before we marry a girl into any family. And here? We don't know how those people live, where they live, or who they are. Nothing. And we sent our daughter away. You have to go. You have to go and make sure they understand that we are not some desperate people who married off our dark daughter to a fair man."*

"What nonsense are you talking, Gowri?!"

"It's not nonsense!" Gowri Devi retorted, *"I am just a grain of a shade darker than you, and do you know how many people said how many things to me when we got married? And Tharani is going to a land where everybody is as fair as a ghost. You should*

go!" she insisted again. *"You should go. They should be made aware of our position and wealth. They will not know that our daughter's marriage was because of divine intervention. They will think that she is a charity case. They..."*

"Gowri!" Swamy admonished, *"You are becoming paranoid. We are sending her with enough gifts to fill a big backyard. What more..."*

Gowri Devi cut him mid-sentence, *"Will you go? Or should I send my brother?"*

Vaibhogam
Thatastu

Coming soon…

"You are being rude, dear," Stanley said, trying not to turn his head lest his butler let out yet another disapproving grunt. "Are you bothered, Geoffrey? by your mistresses' stare?"

"Not in the least, sir." Came the solemn reply. "I understand my lady is merely curious." He did not flinch a muscle in his face. For the past fifteen minutes, Tharani sat keenly observing her husband being dressed by the butler.

"I Am curious." Stated Tharani, "I do not understand why a grown man like you needs another grown man to dress you up?" Tharani asked. The butler maintained his composure.

"Good question. Why do you think, Geoffrey?" Put that way; it presents itself as an unnecessary endeavor." Stanley mused.

The butler cleared his throat. "The gentlemen have other things to do and think off, my lady. They need not be bothered by having to worry about one's attire when they have the workings of an estate to ponder upon." He thought he had provided a reasonable answer.

"Hmm. So you are saying that if a person were to dress themselves, it makes them incapable of thinking about what to do next?"

Geoffrey opened his mouth to answer but did not know what to say. Stanley came to the rescue.

"Continue with your questions, and you will have him worried about his job." He told Tharani, "Thank you, Geoffrey. My lady and I will be down shortly." The butler took his leave and closed the door behind him. Tharani stood up and gave her hand into Stanley's outstretched arm.

"You look splendid, darling." Stanley kissed her hand.

"Thank you." Tharani blushed, glad that she looked presentable. It was not how she had felt an hour ago. The maid who came in to help her offered to do her hair. Problem being that the only way she knew to style any hair was to do it upwards. The length of Tharan's hair was held up at the top of her head, with ringlets falling by the side of her face. Fascinated as she was by the ringlets and the way they framed her face, Tharani did not recognize the woman who stared back from the mirror. Her mother's words rang in her mind. *They have to like you. But you do not have to be like them for them to like you. Do you understand?"*

"No."

"What I am saying is, if you start dressing like them and behaving like them, they will not like Tharani Sri. They like their version of you, not who you really are. Did you understand?"

"No."

Looking at her image now, Tharani had a weird moment of understanding what her mother said. She politely thanked the maid for her efforts. She braided and accessorized her hair with gold extensions from her earrings. A gold and emerald pendant along her forehead matched perfectly with her mustard-colored silk *paavda* and green *voni.* Held snugly against her slender waist with gold *vaddanam.* She was nervous, nonetheless. "You will not leave me alone, will you?" "No"

"*Promise.*" She asked, opening up her palm.

"*Promise.*" Stanley reassured. "I am sorry for what happened today, Tharani...."

She held a finger to his lips. "I should have waited for you to ask me in. I thought she would be happy with the gifts naana sent."

When Stanley was going to respond, a knock on the door revealed the maid. "I am sorry to disturb you, sir. The guests have arrived." She said and bowed her way out.

"Forget what happened. Shall we go?" Tharani asked.

"Of course." Stanley wrapped her arm around his and went out to join the guests.

The ball at Whittamore Mansion was to be the last for the season in the county. Without Stanley's approval of the engagement, Sophia's betrothal could not be announced. Upon receiving word of her son's arrival, Annabelle had planned the ball to ensure things would start rolling into place. His arrival, however, timed perfectly with the ball, and unwillingly, so did the announcement of his new bride. The ballroom broke into loud gasps on the arrival of the Earl and Countess. The first surprise of the earl being married was completely overshadowed by the second. That, the new Lady Whittamore, was not English! Not even European!

"Oh! Who is she?!". "Where is she from?". "Charlie told me he had left for India." "She is wearing a gold waistband!" whispered an old lady. "Did you see her earrings? They extend back into her hair. Upon my word, I have never seen such jewelry! She has a pierced nose, too!" Said another.

"Oh, the silks!" gushed a young girl.

"Do not be so besotted, child!" admonished the girl's mother. "We have a relative that traveled to India. I can very well write to him to bring you some." She said haughtily. "Oh, mama, She looks like a princess!"

"No, she does not." Said lady Rose Dianne Williams. Her face warm and flush with anger, she narrowed her eyes as they followed the earl and his new wife down the room. That should have been her. "I do not see how anybody can find such bright colors of any appeal." She smirked. "All that gold is like a harness holding her down to the ground. Such pompous display..."

"Careful, Rose." A voice warned, "You forget that we are in their house." Baroness Pickering whispered as she sipped her wine. "Your statement reeks of jealousy, my dear. Such manner of talk will have people think that he was the one that broke the engagement."

"He did not!" rebutted Rose. "I did! Which lady of gentle birth would travel around the world in the dust and gravel? "

"Hmm. Be quiet, is all I am saying." She pulled her reluctant daughter to meet the couple. Rose Dianne Williams was Baroness Pickering's second daughter. The baroness, a woman of financial astuteness, saw Stanley as a prime candidate for her wayward second daughter. Having seen how he had responsibly handled the estate, the baroness was happy to push Rose into his path to ensure that her daughter had a healthy house and a steady man by her side. And he was good-looking too. She triumphed when they got engaged and was proud of her sensibility and ability to have both daughters wed into stable, well-to-do households. But that did not last long, as Rose's version of a Lady did not align with Stanley's future. Stanley's proposal was to get married before their departure to India. Rose declined. She did want to get married and take immediate control of the running of the Manor. Not run around in a 'god-forsaken' place. After nearly a month of discussions and arguments, Rose declared that she did not see herself as the lady of Whittamore. Especially after believing that if she could charm Stanley Whittamore, she could charm anybody she set her eyes on. Hence, the engagement was broken, and each made their separate ways. Three years later, Rose did marry for love, as she convinced herself. The charming Mr. Anthony Williams was a strapping young man with a modest dwelling that he slowly built into a prime property. Rose was happy. Until now. She had imagined Stanley would return miserable and lonely, wanting to beg her to be back with him. But that was not the case. He had barely noticed her, as he and his wife walked past them.

"Aunt Betty!" Stanley hugged his mother's younger sister. "I am so happy to see you! I was told you were visiting Hugh." his genuine pleasure made his aunt smile. "May I present my wife? Tharani Sree."

"It is so lovely to see you, too!" her eyes twinkled. She pulled Tharani into the embrace too. "Hello dear. I am your mother-in-law's younger sister." Beatrice Harrington introduced herself to her new niece. "My my, you are a beautiful girl."

Tharani folded her hands in a namaste and bowed her head. "Oh there is no need to be formal. We are a family." Aunt Betty said, "Do you speak English, my dear?"

"I do, Ma'am."

"Call me Aunt Betty." she smiled and then turned to Stanley. "I was visiting Hugh. Had to be back, though, did I not? To meet you and your lovely wife. Oh. And your mother told me what happened this morning," she whispered, leaning towards her nephew.

Stanley raised his brows "She did?" Far across the hall, the dowager sat in a high-backed chair, her place of pride as the matriarchal head of the family. She acknowledged her son's gaze with a haughty snort and turned away to talk to Sophia and Altair, who were flanking her on one side.

"Yes." Beatrice took Tharani's hand in hers. "Trust me when I say this dear, give her time and she will warm up to you. Someone who raised this lovely young man cannot be that bad, now, can they? Did I tell you that Stanley is my favorite nephew?" she asked.

"Thousands of times!" came an exasperated voice from behind them. Robbie came over and kissed his aunt's hand.

"You know I would say the same to your wife." Beatrice smiled and hugged Robbie.

"Of course," Robbie answered.

"I will not keep you. Everybody is waiting to meet the new lady of the house." Beatrice made a wave at the crowd. "I do have to congratulate Sophia and her beau, too." Aunt Beatrice walked to the young couple and shook hands with Altair. Tharani held Stanley's arm as he offered it to her and thus began the round of introductions. As much as they complimented to her face, they left behind a trail of whispers as they walked ahead. Some nice. Some not very nice.

"Baroness Pickering and Ms.Pickering." Stanley introduced. "Theirs is the lovely estate that opens into the county." He said.

"It is Mrs. Williams, actually. But do call me Rose." She extended her hand to Tharani with a curt smile. "You are not the only one to have found marital bliss, Stanley."

Tharani did not miss the eye play and smile that Rose directed at Stanley. *"You know her well?"* Tharani asked, slipping into Telugu.

Stanley cleared his throat "Ms.Pick...Mrs.Williams and I were engaged to be married five years ago."

"We were." Rose cut. She would be the one to tell what actually happened. "Till he decided to move to that hot-as-hell country that I could not bring myself to travel to." she waved her fan to the effect. " I called it off."

Tharani frowned at Rose's derision when speaking of her country. She made herself smile. "Well, I am glad he came. It is hot, but it is a beautiful country."

"I am sure it is. But..." Rose began when her mother cut in, noting Stanley's darkening expression.

"How are you finding England, Mrs.Whittamore? I hope the weather is agreeable to you?"

"It is, ma'am," Tharani replied.

"We should not be keeping you. Others are waiting for the meet and greet, too." the baroness held Rose by the arm and led her away.

"She is pretty," Tharani said. And she was very fair. There were so many fair and good-looking girls around here. All of them were. Hoping for a denial from Stanley, she was disappointed when he chose to remain silent. It, in fact, made her angry. How could he not tell that Rose was indeed not very pretty? That Tharani was prettier. Stanley on the other hand chose not to fuel the spark that Rose left behind. He ignored the question and continued to make introductions and meet his guests.

Meanwhile, on a slightly raised end of the room, Anabelle sat in a decorated high chair, looking over the crowd. Everybody, and more, that she had invited was present. People were having a good time and seemed to be more curious and excited at meeting Stanley and his new wife. She, on the other hand, was excited about the news that was going to be announced. She turned to her sister "I am glad you came by yourself. I do not think I would be able to tolerate that man's presence. Although I do wish you would have allowed me to lend you the pearls Betty " she said taking note of her sister's bear neck.

Annabelle loved her younger sister, which was not the case since their childhood. Beatrice was the prettier girl. But Annabelle was the luckier. It did not take much thought for Annabelle to feel guilty about the kind of blissful marital life that she lived as opposed to the hell hole that her sister was forced into. Mr.Harrington, though a man of title, had little credibility to his name. Something that their father had failed to acknowledge at the time of granting permission to marry his daughter. Despite the late Mr.Whittamore's warning that Harrington did not share a good reputation in the younger circles, Papa Morris was quite firm in his belief that a good marriage would eventually pull a man out of the confusion of his young mind. But that did not happen.

Beatrice patted her sister's hand. "Today is not the day for melancholy, Anna. You have much to celebrate. Your son is back. A new daughter and a new son. They are such lovely young people," her eyes followed Stanley and Tharani. "She is a lovely girl. I understand you are miffed that she is not English but do have some faith in Stanley. He would not have done anything..."

"Of course, he would not!" huffed Anabelle. "It angers me that those people have taken advantage of my son, and now he has to pay for the rest of his life. Who knows what kind of family they are? What does her father do? What sort of family are we associated with now? What blood will my grandchildren carry?"

Beatrice rolled her eyes. "Upon my word, sister! Have you not learned anything? How can you not see that they are happy?"

"They are on their honeymoon, Betty. Once the passion wears off, the true colors will emerge."

"And when will your veil of prejudice lift off?"

" Betty.."

"I will be very disappointed in you, Anabelle if you were to treat that girl any differently than if Stanley were to marry an English girl. I beg of you, please do not let your prejudices overshadow your heart. "

Annabelle hmphed like a young child. "Well, I do wish they would get on with the announcement. How long are my old bones to wait for some cheer.". Just then, Stanley and Tharani made their way to Anabelle. Tharani moved to stand beside Beatrice, avoiding making eye contact with her mother-in-law. Stanley took Sophia's hand and invited Louise to step forward. Turning to the waiting crowd, he spoke loudly and clearly, "Ladies and gentlemen, it is an absolute pleasure to be back in my country and warmly welcomed. You all have been very kind in welcoming the new Mrs.Whittamore. But...Tonight is not about us. You have been invited to join us in our happiness in welcoming Monsieur Louise Altair to our family. He has decided to steal my very dear sister, Ms.Sophia Whittamore, from us. And..I was told I had no choice but to permit that." The crowd laughed and cheered. "So, with the blessings of my mother and me, Altair, she is all yours." Altair bowed his head to Annabelle and Stanley and took Sophia's hands. The young girl blushed as the music flowed, on cue, and Altair pulled her into his arms for a waltz. Other couples joined in. Robert pulled his aunt Beatrice into a dance and had his hand whacked with her fan for the audacity, but she danced nonetheless. Stanley came to stand beside Tharani. "Am I expected to dance?" she asked, seeing the couples switch their partners.

"Yes. I do intend to dance with you, dear. Are you nervous?" He took her hand in his.

"I am." she confessed "But, *will I have to dance with the other men, too?"* her real fear.

Stanley led her to the floor. "You can decline," he said. "Now just like we practiced. Follow my lead." Tharani moved her feet, whispering numbers as she

had learned, "I am happy that you find my shoes to your taste, darling. I am not bad to look at, either."
"Shh. If I listen to you, I will step on your feet."
"If you do not look at me, I will have to kiss you right now," warned Stanley. That got her head jerked up and a laugh from Stanley. "Relax. You dance quite well." Tharani lasted two sets with Stanley, after which she begged to sit with his aunt and mother. Beatrice engaged Tharani in a conversation. Stanley danced with his sisters.

"I cannot believe you dueled with Louise." Sophia was miffed with Stanley.

"I cannot believe you think I would give my sisters away, without a fight. Plus, it is a family tradition." Stanley said with a straight face.

"How would you feel if you had to duel for TArani?" Sophia questioned.

Stanley smiled. "Well, I am already married to her. So, that is a moot point, would you not say?" was the smug reply.

Kalyanam

Thatastu

Bhagya : How can YOU not believe in love?! You loved her din't you?

Sreenadh : No. I thought I loved her . Now I know love does not exists.

Bhagya: It is like saying you don't believe in ghosts because you got scared seeing one !

Betrayed by love once, Sreenadh rules out marriage from his life. He just cannot make that kind of an emotional investment again.

Accused of ruining her father's life. Bhagya decides not to let anybody make or break hers, let alone a husband.

Until fate has them tied in a marriage with an unusual contract.

Also available on Amazon

Kalyanam

www.ingramcontent.com/pod-product-compliance
Lightning Source LLC
Chambersburg PA
CBHW021227130626
46554CB00004B/1402